pornOgraphies

short stories
christopher GRIMES

pornographies

stories by
christopher
GRIMES

Jaded Ibis Press
sustainable literature by digital means.™
an imprint of Jaded Ibis Productions U.S.A.

© 2012 copyright Christopher Grimes

First edition. All rights reserved.

ISBN: 978-0-9831956-5-8
Library of Congress Control Number: 2011937989

Published by Jaded Ibis Press, *sustainable literature by digital means*™ An imprint of Jaded Ibis Productions, LLC, Seattle, Washington USA http://jadedibisproductions.com

Cover and interior art by Scott Zieher. Cover design by Melissa Walker.

This book is also available in digital and fine art limited editions. Visit our website for more information. Excerpts have appeared in Beloit Fiction Journal and KNOCK.

for Maria Luisa Basualdo without whom this book would not have been written

✈ TABLE OF CONTENTS ✦

✈ PREFACE FROM THE PUBLISHER ✦

Contemporary publishing suffers under the unfortunate notion that creative writing (language as art) exists as a *product* to be sold rather than an *idea* to be explored, sometimes repeatedly, to fully understand whatever question or hypothesis first attracted the writer to the ideological territory.

Recall that Montaigne considered his essays (*essais*, literally, *attempts*) as parts of a whole that might never be achieved in one's lifetime. Trying, then — often from many different perspectives, in the same way Gertrude Stein would later write her cubist works — became critical to the development of the idea and the human. "I am myself the matter of my book," said Montaigne. The same is true for any writer, whether of nonfiction, fiction, poetry or hybrid.

Jaded Ibis Press is publishing Christopher Grimes' novel, *The Pornographers*, and his short story collection, *Pornographies*. They are different versions of the same thematic exploration, which is exactly why we are publishing both. Once you and I step outside the tiresome view that books are ultimately consumer goods and must be fixed at some point of "perfection" or else "fail", we rise to a goal much higher than what literature has, sadly, become: We seek to improve the individual, the culture, the society and the species by attempting to understand, through language, the whole as shaped by its parts — much healthier, less corrupt ambition.

I founded Jaded Ibis Press as a necessary "playspace" wherein writers could expand ontological concerns in a way that provides individual and cultural growth; that is, a way to become better humans. Because I am educated in and a practitioner of both creative writing and visual art, my view of what literature might and should be differs from the mainstream and, in most cases, the academy. I do not view a story as a final product but rather one part of a whole that shall only be complete when I die or am otherwise unable or unwilling to intellectually and creatively grow. For example, when exploring the ideas surrounding theoretical physics as it manifests in 2D visuals, I did not create one drawing and then move on to the next topic of exploration. Rather, I created 360 drawings, paintings and mixed media images, stopping only when I felt I'd gained sufficient clarity on a subject that had heretofore compelled me. This method of repeated investigation was a fundamental part of my visual art education; we drew, painted, sculpted and wrote about the same one object for an entire semester or year. The tremendous understanding I gained from the experience continues to inform my professional decisions.

Every book written is an attempt, regardless of what the publishing, marketing and book review industries claim. Knowing and comprehending this fact significantly adds to a reader's intellectual and aesthetic development, for rather than shutting doors before opening another, the reader constructs pathways through a vast and continually expanding library of related information and subsequent processing.

By publishing both versions of Grimes' narrative, Jaded Ibis Press provides readers with a more accurate glimpse into the writer's mind, the human mind, in general, and the history of and future possibilities for human language. We're tremendously excited to have this opportunity to participate in this project.

Debra Di Blasi, Publisher, Jaded Ibis Press
Seattle, Washington, November 2011

WINTER, 2001
✈ THE UNITED STATES OF AMERICA ✦

✈ EVERYBODY WHO DRINKS ✦
THE WATER

Everybody who drinks the water remarks how odorless and tasteless our water is. That the source is an *E. coli*-shy of an open sewer not withstanding, the man hours and expense that goes into our potable H_2O will make your head swim.

Take the cost of just one re-carbonation filter, the re-vulcanization expenditure for a single slag tank next quarter.

This is pretty dry stuff — the base needs of civic life always bores everybody to tears — but the point is we can't keep issuing municipal bonds for basic upkeep, speaking of a direct path to a Moody's downgrading.

You're always on the lookout for creative revenue sources. Taken in this context, our research into online adult entertainment is about as exciting as watching someone do your taxes.

We're talking investment portfolios, long versus short term liquidity, turnover rates, capital trends, coffee breath and bloat.

We're watching with more than passing interest the situation unfolding over there in Salt Lake City, for example, that thing about the video store owner being sued for selling obscene material. We have more than a few video stores in town, so it behooves us not to keep an eye on such developments to get out ahead of them, speaking of salmonella in the salad bar.

What did that mean, *obscene*? The statute, which comes down from the Fed to the State to us, determines that the material is offensive to the average person, applying contemporary community standards — in this case, your average citizen of Salt Lake City.

The lawsuit was finally dropped.

The guy's averaging four thousand adult video sales a month.

Not bad, four thousand videos, but the citizens of Salt Lake are buying five times that much through cable, satellite and the Internet. Just what did this say about the community standard? Exactly.

The point here is that the whole thing catches the attention of our Comptroller, who did a little investigating of his own and reported back to us. It turns out that over 50 percent of those staying in hotel rooms that offer pay-per-view buy an adult feature. That's just the beginning.

The numbers are staggering.

We're talking a $10 billion dollar annual industry in the United States alone, with a potential for a 377% profit margin.

We're talking supremely quick turnover.

No way, Jose, someone interrupts at this point, we're not going down that road. Immediately there's a default consensus against the idea, naturally, a certain Protestant repulsion to an open display of T&A, to say nothing of being in anyway implicated in the cinematic conjoining of the genitalia, so to speak.

Let him talk, someone says, meaning the Comptroller.

General Motors, he says, AT&T, we're not talking some sleazeball operation with a storefront in a strip mall, not that there's anything wrong with strip malls per se. We're talking companies headed by Mitt Romney and Rupert Murdoch. Do we have a problem being in that company?

Here's the clincher: There's just no way *not* to make money hand over fist. There's just not.

We're not talking long-term investment, either. It's not like you call up some guy in Reno and fork over a couple hundred thousand and wait, hoping he doesn't disappear in a rusted El Camino into the desert.

You buy AT&T stock for their Hot Network. Through DIRECTV, GM sells more sex flicks than Larry Flynt.

You got a problem buying GM stock? Hilton, Comcast, Marriott International?

Give us a break. Just like that, the consensus swings in the opposite direction. We're in.

The point is, this is just a taste of the behind-the-scenes decision-making that happens daily in municipal government of which your average citizen is happily unaware.

Take our strict ordinances on signage, for example. It keeps up certain appearances that, although you'd be hard pressed to put your finger on it, everyone calls *nice*.

That's the effect.

The secret's no neon.

No one would know enough to ask about it, nor should they, really, nor, to give another example, that our building codes prohibit the erection of a structure more than four stories high. Our soil is super rich and loamy, not at all suited for bearing the stress and footprint of tall buildings.

Everything's therefore built to moderate scale.

In this way, our homes look genuinely homey.

Modesty is our policy. Bring the family, stay for the day, stay for the rest of your goddamned life, right?

Our motto: You're welcome!

This should be an official Mayoral address, wherein we acknowledge that we lacked for little if anything in the old days.

Time changes every single thing.

✈ NOW CONSIDER CALAMITY ✦ MITIGATION

Now consider calamity mitigation, the costs thereof, it'll make your nose bleed, what with Hazmat suits at $550 per, not including breathing apparatus, not including boots, not including disaster control or the appropriate vehicles to get you on-scene in a manner befitting.

Think it's easy? Think those detonation robots come cheap? A suspicious something shows up and needs blowing up per regulation. What are you supposed to do, *borrow* one?

You have to think of your own, is the point.

You play the hand you're dealt. Our Chamber of Commerce is making no apologies at present for it, though the Rotarian faction in particular will want it said that we hadn't been going around looking for capital investments in online adult entertainment.

But when the idea presented itself we took it up, our hand, just as it was dealt. We are in need of *so* many things. Anti-burn aerosols, trauma pads, a Kenworth 32-foot T300 Mobile Control and Command Center equipped with limited slip-locking differential brakes, Jacobs Extarder, 5-speed automatic transmission, one-touch electric awning, street side workstations, overhead storage cabinets, hinged dry erase locking boards, removable task swivel chairs, drop-in insertable conference table, bulkhead divider with sliding doors, Kenmore microwave, Sanyo refrigerator, Black & Decker 12 Cup Spacemaker Coffee Maker, four 32-inch Sharp LCD TVs, a Sony DVD/VCR player, Hughes receiver, HP All-In-One color printer, Ratheon IR-360 Dual Camera (including thermal and night vision systems), Shurflo Extreme

5.7 gallons per minute water pump, 30-gallon fresh and gray water tanks, Kenwood Marine speakers, Phone Patch Block EVI, Tellular Phone Cell Fixed Wireless Terminal, Orion All-In-One Weather Station, dual battery selector switch, 120/240 Marathon Diesel power generator, Moto-Sat 1.2 meter Internet satellite and KVH Trac Vision #S3 Mobile Digital Satellite dishes, all tricked out in neon green, preferably, to match the other vehicles in our Emergency Management fleet, because we *need* one, because we have to start thinking of our own and play the hand we're dealt, a hand we should make no apologies for playing,

We have nothing to hide.

Our community leadership strives for transparency such as this.

Public relations advises full disclosure. And you know what, we're *glad*.

Here's your headline: *Mayor stands firm* [in his conviction that he continues to speak the interests of the people]. The buck stops here, he announces, so if some young potato spud from the *Shopper*, or anywhere else for that matter, thinks there's a scoop here, there's not.

We stand united behind him, the Mayor, most of us. Even the women's yoga faction can't actually be said to be against us, despite the noises they're making to the contrary. The fact is, they've been planning their trip to India for some time, and given the recent prohibitions on air travel, they're using the moment to press their original itinerary.

It's manipulation is what it is, but now, every time an aircraft passes overhead, we're forced to look up at it and wonder how, if they actually left, we'd be standing here, looking up and longing for their return — such is our abiding love and worry for them — just standing here, hoping that they'll be home shortly.

✈ IT'S A FACT ✦

It's a fact. We weren't prepared. One moment it's business as usual, and the next, the *The Price is Right* is pre-empted by the now familiar images of the World Trade Center on fire.

It's unbelievable, of course. Who can forget it? The clips of the airplanes penetrating the towers, the repeating shots of fiery jet fuel spraying out of them. And then how one directly after another, it seemed, they collapsed, imploding onto themselves, into a massive cloud of dust, and when that, too, was spent, how we all saw that the towers vanished, were gone.

Predictably, several of us wanted immediate and violent revenge, but then it wasn't at all clear who was to blame. The Russians? Deranged passengers? FAA hardware? There was Oklahoma to consider.

There was a lot of yawning, as if the truth of the images was too exhausting to take in all at once. It was a terrible day, as everybody knows.

A response was hard to come by, and after it did finally come, the fiscal response to support it was even more difficult. It was only later that one of us stumbled on the Pew statistics — re: adult entertainment venues vis-à-vis Internet — prompting the initial research, which revealed in a nutshell that as successful pornography is made into something always already known by the general consuming public, specialized productions tend to disappear from view. What's the point here?

The point was to keep it simple. It got us thinking.

You can't over-think these things, is the point.

The so-called *money shot*, for example, is and always will be the money shot, we discovered. That's why it's called the *money shot*. You can't improve upon it — the mandatory sign of sexual climax, a compulsory indication that pleasure is achieved.

Further research firmly indicated that what was true on VHS in the 1980s and 90s holds true in today's online environments, perhaps even more so. In fact, our research suggested increased investment in the money shot.

In fact, if resources were limited, as they so clearly are, it was apparent to us that we could forget everything else that we might discover and let it *all* ride on the money shot.

From there, we worked very hard at feeling our way through the basic rules of the form, the way female ejaculations, to give one instance, were depicted in no more than six percent of all money shots sampled. And of all figures presented in advertising adult sites, a full 72 percent are female. More specifically, these women are thin (98%), young (92%), white (66%) and have long (84%) and blonde (48%) hair. Male figures were usually present only as phallus, with the rest of the male body, especially the head, framed out.

Also acts marketed as lesbian — we mean girl-on-girl scenes here — were typically choreographed to suggest the possibility of the male consumer joining it, i.e., the female performers, usually highly feminine, performing fellatio on dildos while gazing toward the camera. In other words, this act (fallatio) was meant to imply the penis, or penis-like object, as the assumed source of pleasure in lesbian sex while reminding the recipient of the power of his own peanut.

Our research revealed that, for promotional purposes, description of women most often included *girl* (31%), *slut* (22%), *babe* (10%) and *lesbian* (7%), described variously as *hot* (33%), *teen* (22%), *sexy* (9%), *young* (9%), *nasty* (4%), *sweet* (3%) and *innocent* (3%). References to men, on the other hand, were weighted as follows: *guys* (64%), *men* (10%), *studs* (8%), *mates* (6%), *buddies* (4%), *dudes* (4%) and *brothers* (2%). Descriptions for the male genitalia included *big* (45%), *monster* (17%), *huge* (12%), *over 12 inches* (9%), *fat* or its synonym *thick* (8%) and *massive* (4%). In contrast, the descriptor and frequency of female genitalia included *tight* (73%), *tiny* (11%), *little* (8%) and *small* (8%).

Then there were the trends that we were noticing, especially the emergence of sites dedicated to the genre of the first person point of view — more specifically, the increasingly pervasive employment of digital cameras, which are held by the receiver of the sex act, and therefore mimic the point of view of the one being serviced. We figure there's going to be a continued push in thi first person effect. We mean, take *Suck Me Slut*, for example, which has experienced the kind of success that all of us are looking for. The camera is in the hands of the male performers, but the men are visible only as their genitalia, hands and legs.

This directly corresponds to the emphasis placed upon the marketing phrase *cock worship* in *Suck Me Slut*'s content description, and how it's evident in the image gallery: licking and sucking male genitalia or pushing a penis down one's throat are depicted as expressions of female desire. The impression is maintained in images of women looking up to the camera and closing their eyes in enjoyment while men ejaculate on their faces.

And finally there was the discovery of the unalterable truth, not to be fiddled with in any way, shape or form, which is that the simplicity of the story, the simplicity of the *pornography* story, it bears repeating over and over and over again, cannot be overemphasized. Our research revealed that, as it has always been in mainstream culture, arousal is achieved best through the use of stock characters, since complex and contradictory characters evoking different kinds of emotions tend to decrease and disturb the experience.

Stock characters and settings enable quick transition to the act itself.

Meaning, once the scene is set we can get down to the real action.

Word to the wise, we remind ourselves: while templates produce a certain degree of repetition and familiarity, they do not dictate the content or meaning of the experience in question. That would be our job.

✈ AFTER THE ATTACK ON THE ✈ UNITED STATES OF AMERICA

After the attack on the United States of America, we noticed that things were getting pretty tense on the home front. There was the attack itself, which was brutal enough, but add to that staffing shortages at the DNR, the inability to find a comfortable sleeping position in your last trimester, one count of embezzlement, asbestos found in the old Brachs candy factory condo development, lost retainers at $225 a pop, health insurance policies denying coverage for physical therapy, budget deficits at the municipal, state and federal levels, another heart attack in the ranks, threats of celibacy, a melanoma, life.

A lot of us booked rooms at the hotel with the Jacuzzis, but that's just one night, as nice a night as it was.

It was a confusing and turbulent time. There was nothing normal about it.

One of the bigger sources of contention was our moratorium on air travel, which was met by a majority of the women with some hostility. Their plans for air travel were a full eight months in the making. That was just too bad. Our position was no air travel under any circumstances. A majority of the women's position was that we shut up and shove our position.

We turned now to the relationship advice we'd begun compiling in earnest.

Bottom line, we said, speaking of hostile phrases, it needs to be said here that inasmuch as shutting up doesn't really provide a neutral blank for its intended receiver to fill, we should agree to just go ahead and skip that sort of thing, the telling of someone to shut up, for example.

Because if we've learned anything, shouldn't we have learned to be a little nicer to each other? we asked. Because if all it took was shutting up, that'd be easy, wouldn't it.

Notice this was not a question.

Who famously said that one can only and always speak for oneself?

It's unimportant.

Fundamentally, the women's position was that the problem was not *when* to shut up but rather not being able to *make* someone shut up, not now, not here, not *ever*.

Question: Was this supposed to be a professional diagnosis?

It probably wasn't meant to be a professional diagnosis.

Because, we said, this didn't sound so much like a professional diagnosis as a personal opinion.

Here was another example of a professional diagnosis we remember being floated around at this time, that the pregnant women shouldn't intercourse when they're pregnant.

That was definitely a personal opinion because, in fact, it *is* advisable to intercourse when you're pregnant, as we now well know, plus the fact that the current literature suggests that it gets the old mud flowing.

The pregnant women in particular were forbidden to travel for obvious reasons. Still, they wanted to join the non-pregnant women, who were also forbidden to travel.

Unfortunately, the women in general had to cancel their so-called yoga retreat, which really was unfortunate. Their final destination, a scummy little industrial town in the south of India, a real toilet, where some gnome in a Speedo and Rolex would be paid pretty handsomely to spank their Spandexed asses.

We saw the promotional DVD. Obviously, we now said, absolutely not.

We reminded them that our country is at war. We reminded them that it wasn't us who plotted and executed such heinous acts, and that they needed to open their eyes and see things the way they were, that our country was at *war*, for Christ's sake.

Plus, don't forget the anthrax being express mailed into our breakfast cereal.

Just look around, we said, people are *dying*.

Then one of us floated an example of what was later described as a highly negative personal opinion. Well screw it, it started, so you could tell from the get-go that the so-called well was being poisoned, which, to be honest, we were advised against doing from the research we'd been compiling.

Specifically, the opinion was that maybe we should *all* up and join some clit-flicking commune.

It's here that the women interjected. Just to be clear, they said, this was meant specifically for the odd asshole among us, that is, if the odd asshole among us could agree to call words by their particular, proper nouns, if that were possible: It's called an *ashram*, they said, not to get too technical about it.

It was the beginning of a pretty hot dressing-down, and we sought out some more objective opinions fast in order to defend ourselves against it, the attack, which finally came, a defense.

The physiological and psychological benefits of yoga were not at issue here, someone finally fired off, however important these benefits might be.

That's maybe a better question than a statement, we thought, but what the hell, at the risk of sounding repetitious, regardless, okay, so that issue was off the table.

If we'd learned anything, one of us continued, hadn't we learned that life is fragile?

That might be spot-on, one of us said, but listen, somebody better get a little something pretty quick around here, or somebody around here is out of here.

In retrospect, that seemed a pretty unfortunate position for us to take.

The women in general restated their vow of celibacy at this point. It was particularly hilarious coming from the pregnant women. They'd been forwarding to each other a mass-mailer put out by some organization that billed itself the Women's World Wide Peace Movement, subject line *No Peace, No Pussy*. A normal human being just deletes a subject line like that, but they didn't, no. It's a big deal at the time.

The general advice on the matter indicated that it was important for us to value one standing by her convictions, otherwise speech is just so much flatulence.

✈ WE RECONVENED ⤺

We reconvened on email pretty often around now, not just to discuss our evolving business plan (already amply demonstrated by this time) but also to continue to work what we termed the yoga problem, which we'd been investigating in fits and starts for over a year now. Given the renewed sense of urgency, we doubled our efforts. The preliminary findings were finally starting to come in. That said, it was suggested by a large minority that we might be better served by furthering our research into the former (online porn) rather than the latter (yoga).

Considering the problems we were having on the home front, though, and the fact that the preliminary findings were coming in, most thought it best to re-prioritize.

We'd get back to the core marketing issues soon enough. The thinking about the adult website was pretty primitive, but we were encouraged by the notion that once up it would be self-sustaining, so we could buy ourselves some time here. All we really had to do is think through the issue of cross-positing, how to keep some dipshit in Scottsdale from trying to horn-in and post images of his Jeep Cherokee for sale.

Here then began an exposition on the yoga, the ancient instruction manuals for which are translated from the Sanskrit, written in the form of sutras and read, we knew, by the women.

The Sanskrit word sutra is the English thread, such that sutures derive from sutras.

Yoga means union [n], or to yoke [v].

Apparently Hindi historians date the Sanskrit aphorisms collected in The

Yoga Sutras of Patanjali at 500 B.C. to 200 B.C.

Sri Swami Satchidanada of the Satchidanada Ashram (Yogaville, Virginia) fixes their date somewhere between 5000 B.C. and 300 B.C., but he is suspected by his peers of exaggerating in order to elevate his own situation.

Swamis in general seem unified against the subversive ego, this infamous I of ours, described variously as a Velcro to pleasure, swooning diva in pain, terrified Box Terrier snarling at death, clinging sloth to the tree of life, and therefore source of our misery.

Be death, the swami says, pansy.

I am a big fat pansy, the swami says, and the pansy's bed, the sky in which the pansies bloom, a #2 sheet rock screw lodged in a steel-belted Firestone Wilderness radial tire, the tire itself, the truck.

Our lives are inferential, the swami says, illusory, so that we are all of us a steaming pile of spoor from which we are to infer the animal browsing conifers in the blue silence of a cold winter night, the conifers themselves, the animal, the blue silence, the winter, the cold.

It was all a little more flowery than most of us were used to, but judging from the lack of knee-jerk response to the initial findings, it was met with due consideration.

Someone broke in for a weather check here, which meant that things were wrapping up. The present weather at that time was 47 degrees Fahrenheit, an unseasonably warm December afternoon in the Midwestern region of the United States of America.

47 degrees — it was something!

However, the pressure was falling. An artic front was barreling down from Alberta, Canada. Blizzard conditions were expected overnight.

But today, the sky was a dim grey, the air uncommonly thick and soft, like your head was in a box of cotton. It's so silent in fact that someone remarked that you could almost hear the oncoming snow.

Then someone suggested the phrase baleful moaning. There were a lot of laughs out louds at that, and then we convened.

✈ WE'LL TAKE CONTROL ✦

We'll take control over the necessary space to pursue our online entertainment interest on the DNR's server in January or February, maybe March at the latest. This was the current thinking at the time. We were looking at a 1.5 million dollar deficit.

We're talking a CP 750 Whisper fresh out of the crate. That was some muscle back in the day. Today, no, but a half year ago? You better believe it.

The DNR doesn't even know what to do with it. We're waiting on the software that's supposed to be coming down from the State. Take your requisition to get the copier fixed at the Courthouse, and quadruple it, times a factor of ten.

Meanwhile, the thing was just sitting there silent, gathering flies, so to speak.

The way we figured it, we'd use it to see if we could get enough cash flow going to roll it over and buy another dedicated server to replace the one we were using.

The thing's just sitting there, for Christ's sake, week after week, collecting dust.

That's probably pretty clear at this point.

It should be mentioned here that this was done with the women's explicit consent, more or less. They, the women, they're some real what's-good-for-the-goose-is-good-for-the-gander gals, meaning so-called equal opportunists, mostly, the women. It's precisely because most of them don't work in government that we rely on them to advise us when government is working well for them and when it's not.

Other than ourselves, they, more than anyone else, know the full scope of the deficits we're made to labor under.

So we floated our little web hosting interest in a series of what you might call informal presentations over the course of the fall and they finally said show us.

Basically we said okay, sit down. Here's what we're going to do and here's how were going to do it.

They wanted specifics.

Here's what we're talking about, we said, sat them in front of the computer, typed in the address for *Hot Sexxx* and lit it up.

They said: How much. It's not a question.

How much to get in? Or how much can we make?

How about both, they said.

They're no dummies. We're still burning from not buying Microsoft stock. Some friends of friends bought back when they had a couple of hundred people on payroll and just had their IPO.

Micro-what, right?

We for one didn't, meaning, buy.

The next intermittent windshield wiper is wiping the windshield right before our eyes, slow and steady, dragging itself back and forth, back and forth, slowly, right before our eyes. You just need to see it. So you got to keep your eyes open and see it is the point.

Why didn't we put a little money in Yahoo? What kind of name's Google, anyway? It's not fair. We didn't know.

The smart sonofabitches are keeping the big deals under wraps, that's why. How they do this is by distraction. Take the clocks resetting, that whole Y2K business about a memory conniption coming from mixing up the 0s and 1s in the code. The fact is the resetting of the clocks is a simple operation, almost mechanical, requiring such a small amount of memory that you can't hardly speak of it as memory at all. So Y2K comes and goes, no problem.

Big surprise, the doomsayers say that the big catastrophe was really going to happen at the end of '01, seeing that it didn't happen on New Years 2000 like they already promised it would.

Meanwhile, there's the attack on the United States of America. Remember that.

This probably sounds like one of those conspiracy theories, but that whole memory and clock-setting business looks like a pretty carefully orchestrated distraction, as if one catastrophe could outweigh and detract from the other. The problem here is that the clocks resetting catastrophe was nothing, no matter how much everybody wanted it to be more.

The point is they keep us from paying attention to the right thing so they can keep it for themselves, the right thing, and then when it's obvious that it's right in front of you all the time, it's a little too late. Surprise. Look it.

The women say let's talk about this later.

We were being humored, we knew it, but we didn't care. Off they go with their hemp bloomers to practice breathing and god knows what, leaving us to stare into the closing window of a four-billion-dollar-a-year industry.

You take your basic refrigerator packing material and cut it up and sell it for twenty-five bucks as a so-called sticky mat what costs you for free to begin with. Now that's a hell of a racket that we should've bought into in the first place, speaking of fiscal responsibility, of getting in when the getting's good.

We're late to the party already, but the party's still going.

Just then the biggest headache was thinking through our financial transactions, which, at least for now, are handled by a third-party vendor.

They want their cut.

You can't blame them. It's a free market economy, so that's how it goes. Still, there's a lot of money to be made if you can bring to market a better way to handle these transactions, which has really got us thinking. If a push of the button can empty out an entire airspace, how come we can't process a $21.50 membership fee for ourselves? That's the buzz.

That's what we wanted to know.

✈ IT WAS SUBTLE AT FIRST ✈

It was subtle at first, but the women started calling each other different names at about this point. It took us a while to realize that they were talking about themselves when they used them.

What happened is that their so-called swami had assigned them different names to call themselves. It took us a little while to catch on, but we caught on, eventually.

It was a pretty confusing and turbulent time.

At first you'd hear them on the phone and they'd drop a name you'd never heard — Anandi or Suprita or Spatula — but you didn't think a thing about it. Maybe they were talking about someone's aunt in Toledo.

Who cares.

But then it got to the point where you didn't know who they were talking to or who they were talking about, and after they hung up the phone, you'd say who's that? And they'd tell you Sharvina. And you'd say who's that? And they'd give you the perfectly good English name that you've known her by all your life, and you'd say *oh*, for lack of anything else to say, until you thought it through for a second, and then you'd say *what*? *Why*?

The jig was up. That swami of theirs was really throwing the net out now, it seemed to us, and the women were swimming right into it. But why? we wanted to know. What's this guy up to? Knock it off, we said to the women, Stop it.

Stop what?

Stop this name-calling business.

It's nothing serious, they said.

If it's nothing serious, we reasoned, then stop it. It's annoying.

Annoying how? It's *annoying*.

Couldn't they see how annoying it was? Couldn't they act normal for one second?

Plus, what was this swami bastard's intention, exactly?

We found out soon enough. Despite everything — despite the current state of affairs on the home front, despite all of our appeals to reason — they were going to India.

They had never canceled their reservations.

They had never asked for their money back. They were going, they said.

You're not going, we said, and then things got pretty still. We were prepared for screaming and maybe something more, something physical, even. The stillness was spooky. It was quiet and unnerving.

After a while, you just kind of backed out of the room.

In the garage, the Giants were playing the Packers on the radio. You had a few beers and sorted screws, biding time, waiting it out.

It was the beginning of a long night.

It's too tiring just to think about it.

✈ STRESS ✦

Stress issues became a factor around this time — the ability to pace for hours, the staring into the distance, the obsessive whistling, which could drive everyone batty.

If that didn't work, if stress became panic, there's the quick dissolve dose of Clonazepam to consider, but this had to be considered sooner in the stress related event than later, ideally *before* the onset of the panic event, meaning preemptively, meaning the use of the Clonazepam had to be administered, in the words of the prescriber, *prophylactically.* This required a certain measure of self-care.

You needed to understand when, however subconsciously, your own best interests were under attack, despite one's apparent inability to identify moments when one's own best interest were under attack. We were warned of that.

We blamed this stress primarily on the terrorists. But there was also the looming budget crisis and the general low-level anxiety involved in starting our business venture. It all adds up.

Probably a really shitty example of self-care that we blamed on the terrorists is one that involved dragging out the big red cooler from the garage into the sunlight, filling it, the big red cooler, with ice and a twelve pack of Coors before noon in order to scrape and prime the trim on the house.

That's a really good example of negative self-care.

That basically gets you a fall off the ladder, down into the hydrangeas, which were just now in bloom, and which were now crushed, now totally ruined.

How much beer was consumed in this example?

There's still ice in the cooler, more than enough to fill a Ziplock Freezer Bag, but otherwise the cooler's empty, which earned a big F-minus on the self-care report card.

That's a really poor example of self-care.

That gets you writhing on the dining room floor with a dislocated shoulder. There were a lot of questions.

Exactly how much beer was left at this point?

There must have been a lot of spillage, so to speak, and then there was some passing out on the dining room floor from the pain.

It was very stressful. There was the stress at work, the Arabs attacking our homeland, land surveys for emergency staging areas with triage tents, the risk of starting our new business to support such efforts. You could get the whole thing up and working, and then you just had to pray for positive activity.

What it is is fishing. You throw your bait out there, and just like fishing, you can see the nibble on the bait, the interested hits, the passers-by, but if no one is swallowing, you change baits. That's how it works, more or less. You throw out a little *deep throat* action, a little *blonde nubile deep throat action*, switching things around, a little *missionary* now and then to catch the so-called traditionalists, which, by the way, there's no such thing to speak of, if there ever was such a thing.

That pool's run pretty well bone-dry.

✈ WHAT WE SHOULD DO ✦

What we should do is tell what we know, some of us were already thinking, meaning an unexploited revenue stream existed in selling what we already know about the online adult entertainment business.

In other words, we could position ourselves as consultants.

First we would say how happy we are to be here with you, talking about interfaces, the web hosting and the whatnot. We'd say that this was really exciting venue for us, whatever this venue was, and, frankly, speaking from outside the beltway, we find this all really fascinating, meaning, again, whatever venue we were speaking in.

The point is to emphasize the outside-the-beltway perspective, the outsider perspective, that's our angle

Then a joke: Hey, is this what you people actually do for a living? Ha ha! A joke, people, really. Seriously, though, fascinating, fascinating stuff.

We're working at this point with the program one of us had lately survived first-hand when accompanying his wife to one of her own seminars. So we say: You can count on us to hang back for the Hindi iconography in Led Zepplin lyrics, as what comes after the lunch break, and also here on the program something about the meaning of breathing and the right ways of jumping. Is that right? We were really big fans of the Led Zepplin lyrics, way back before we got married, when we were just a bunch of snot-nosed teenagers, so really, this is our lucky, lucky day, to say nothing about the breathing. Jumping, we're not so sure of, but okay, we're willing to learn a little something here today, in so far as jumping is concerned.

It's a pretty complicated program, speaking of programs.

Now it's on to this morning's topic.

Here's where we get down to business.

Some of us had been working on it pretty hard lately.

It begins with the fact that it's common knowledge in certain circles that the platforms available to us at the Department of Natural Resources — as well as those operated by most state and federal agencies for that matter — provide an abundance of feral spaces for the development of commercial online adult entertainment sites. This has to do with the government's tendency to both invest in surpluses and to think about communication traffic as a measure of volume, i.e., *bigness*. In this way, the United States government has unwittingly become the largest exporter of Internet pornography in the entire world.

We're not saying which DNR, of course. We're not giving that information away. But we don't want to be too cagey, either, and lose the practical gist of the point of the information. But to be perfectly clear here, we're not talking *piracy* but *opportunity*.

It's become a tricky business. Times are changing. Historically, Internet pornography sites made their profit exclusively by selling subscriptions to content. A worrisome trend, however — we worry about this all the time, believe it — is that much in the same way gas station owners don't make their money from the pump but from the overpriced sundries sold as conveniences, adult entertainment sites are being made to rely more and more on the sale of various male enhancement and sexual performance drugs, as well as an array of prosthetic devices, primarily vaginas of a synthetic material, assorted vibrators and your classic polymer dildos.

Competition has recently dictated that much of the content the consumer was required to purchase in the past is made available for free in so-called promotional material: Advertising revenue, another, though less crucial, profit source, is based on the amount of traffic through a given site, not on the quality of the consumer's experience. The hit's a cash register ring, people. You remember that.

The frustration for the upstart webmaster in such places as our local

Department of Natural Resources, to take our example, is that the DNR is not a warehouse facility, naturally, and that accumulating and processing large amounts of merchandise would undoubtedly call attention to oneself and such so-called ancillary enterprises.

Despite these frustrations, we believe that there is no better time to get into the business. The attack on the United States of America has resulted in a surge in Internet pornography traffic. We've seen triple-digit growth in the quarter beginning September and ending this past November, 2001, which should be a surprise to no one, considering that Americans are becoming pretty bored with the increased amount of time they are spending at home — restaurant receipts are down a dismal 11.6% nationwide — and also because pornography in general has been shown to relieve stress, the stress-reducing effects having been long established in the scientific community (idea: pop-up survey asking consumer to comment on motive for visiting *à la Expedia*).

As usual, the downward pressure on the industry comes from those who hold tenaciously to their non-masturbatory, what we call, *mythologies*. Meaning, all the available studies show if you put a typically but not exclusively male someone in a room with a computer for a week, and you assure them of their privacy, the first thing they're going to do is email. The second thing their going to do is access a little online porn. This is true from Atlanta to Zimbabwe. The patterns of our inquiries and searching is nearly identical, regardless of culture. In as much as the content of the Internet and its usage is made from our minds, it's hard to deny we're not of the same mind (pause for laughter), regardless of culture. Except for the Japanese. Those Japanese statistically speaking are the most undersexed people in the world. They're also the largest consumers of Internet pornography in the world. You do the math.

First we want to talk, then we want to see a little skin.

In that order.

The rest of our usage — everything from shopping to research — is pretty well dwarfed by email and porn.

Question: What about games?

We are not here to apologize for this truth. We're here to remind you all, who said it, somebody famous, that all of it — the movies, the books, the songs on the radio, the paintings, the TV shows — all of it's about three things: the birth, the sex, the death. That's the way it is. We're born, we shoot our wad, and then we fall down and die. In between we do a lot of taking and thinking about these things, although we probably wouldn't use the phrase *shoot our wad*, per se.

As far as we're concerned, the sex act itself as offered by your basic Internet pornography provider offers the whole production in miniature. You got your foreplay, you got the climax at the climax, as it were, and then you got your satisfied sleep, or whatever, as it happens off-camera. We don't apologize for what we can't change. It's simply the way we're built, all of us. We are entertainment providers. This is the unquestionably the future.

In closing we would like to distribute some tasteful brochures, ones with the slots cut in them for business cards.

➤ WE POOLED OUR RESOURCES ➤

We pooled our resources around this time and arranged for one of us to meet with a marriage counselor in order to mine information and then to report back. In a modestly long and uncelebrated career, the marriage counselor said — we're paraphrasing — one comes to the inescapable conclusion that what appears to be a spectacular occurrence is the end result of commonplace occurrences, habituated over time, going thusly unnoticed as habits are wont to do: an inequitable division of domestic labor, for example, is apparently a biggie.

So while you might think housework is divided pretty equitably in your home, your spouse might beg to differ. You might claim to help with the laundry, for example, but then what does *help* mean here? You might actually do all the laundry, and the dishes, too — the breakfast dishes, lunch dishes *and* the dinner dishes, for example, or you might do the drying of the clothes but not the washing of the clothes, so in point of fact you are not doing the laundry *in toto*, in as much as the laundry requires both the washing and the drying of the clothes.

A marriage is a negotiation. Your spouse might have a thing about drying the clothes, the same thing your spouse has about washing silverware, something about the sound of metal on metal — forks against spoons, zippers against the dryer drum — that, your spouse swears, *hurts the teeth*. So you dry the previously washed clothes but, fuck it, the clothes must be folded for the laundry to be *done*, properly speaking, so perhaps you get roped into doing that, too. A sink full of silverware means that the dishes haven't been washed, properly speaking, so perhaps you get roped into doing that, too.

Quite democratic of you.

You fold the clothes democratically, meaning that you fold your clothes and you fold your spouse's clothes, and perhaps you fold anything else that happens to need folding, despite what your spouse might say. Her clothes are almost precious in their smallness, inasmuch as it's impossible not to be moved while folding them. Holding them up, you almost can't believe that they fit an adult human being. Her little shirts, her little pants and washable skirts — the size of her panties, some of them cotton, some of them silk, some with faded stripes, some of them slippery, shiny and new — they are all deeply moving in their extraordinarily vulnerable, solitary smallness.

Some basic assurances, the marriage counselor generally advised, that's what the women appeared to want, as if we're falling from a burning building, as if the flames and smoke behind us are so unbearably intense that the only decision is to jump, do we think we could hold the women's hands? Despite our fear of heights? Despite every anxiety dream of being stranded on high, unstable places, could all our affections be marshaled in resisting the most deeply felt and primitive impulse to let go and hide our face with the fingers of our hands before impact, regardless of how futile this gesture would be, even if we're such a great distance to the ground and therefore twisting in the wind above or below each other for a full six or seven seconds, depending on cross winds, so that our shoulders are ripped from their sockets, our hold on each other an agony of pain? Given all of this, could we still not let each other go and be included in such an example?

✈ INTERPRETING THE ✦ MEN'S ACTIONS

Interpreting the men's actions required us to take a step back for a moment now, and when we stepped back we realized we needed more input than our collective capacities allowed, so we enlisted even more professional resources, one of which suggested the article used before the word *men* to indicate a growing and much needed distance, an objective assessment — the men as objects, in other words — as if the men could be seen at once inside and outside their relationship to other objects, assembled matters of unadorned facts: The men whose hands were cupped around their women's swollen bellies, trying to feel the subtle movement, the little twitter and thrum promised there, abruptly stood and denounced any other man who would do them and theirs harm. The men as a gaping silences on the declaration after delivering it — the denouncement (not a word about the babies' movements, however; we're still waiting on that good news, gentlemen!) — earnestly speechless afterwards (there's a lot of stammering) but undoubtedly soldiering on toward a speakable language in the layers of images occupying their minds (read: professional research hazard), unbelievable amounts of fluid erupting like geysers from various vaginas mostly (a newly emergent category and, as such, a marketing preoccupation, though it was already subdivided between shaved and unshaved sources), plus the mountains of limbs, the various shadows on inestimable amounts of flesh, the bottomless, black orifices — anal, oral, vaginal, orbital — all thinly veiled in a fog of smoke, originating from an unimaginable fire burning somewhere unseen.

What is known is that the firemen were still unable to put the fire out somewhere.

Otherwise, why still the smoke?

There was also a solitary shovel somewhere in there, sticking up from the dirt garden that the men had been hacking at all week long in their respective back yards.

Here's a little advice for the novice gardener: A little peat makes the carrots grow!

It was equally important that we attempted to make some of the women's positions known here, the professional resource advised, despite the benefits they may have accrued from them.

What the world wanted now more than ever, it's clear to us, was practical realists.

Forthwith, we recognized that the so-called bikini wax indulged a man's pedophiliac fantasies, and that the aggressively baggy clothes worn by our young people of late was an attempt to be seen as infantile, children playing dress up in big people's clothes and therefore not responsible for their increasingly unglued lives (well, it was time to grow up, wasn't it, you little shits?) — and, finally, gestation had been the subject of some of the men's children, with or without their elaboration. Meaning, we admitted it, some of us need to shut up a little bit more and do some listening.

We *heard* these concerns, and we had already taken the following measures, well before the women raised them, their concerns, in the first place. We were no longer considering cross-posting material from *Captain Stabbin',* with its claim (albeit gimmicky and undoubtedly staged) that the *crew* is thrown overboard after *getting it in the end.*

We have always been closed to the *Pregnant Moms* category, as well as to all forms of bestiality and any suggestion whatsoever of minors, including the simple designation *17.*

Several of us have been considering joining Big Brothers in an effort to generate some positive self-esteem in our more wayward, baggy youths.

✈ WATCH US END UP ❌
ON 60 MINUTES

Watch us end up on *60 Minutes*, one of us said around this time.

The Mayor's press secretary lost a little color at the mention of it, looked, for a second, like a boiled kohlrabi, the word *blanched*. Then his color returned and he became a little flushed. Bring it on, he said, and then commenced to draft a letter on the spot, actually *informing* the television news magazine of our online adult entertainment enterprise, if and when we actually produced it. The letter would be sent at the first sign of trouble.

That's what we mean when we say we're getting out in front of it:

Our Mayor sitting down with Ed Bradley, the lighting always looking like they're inside a supper club, but in the background you'd see the thing itself, the CP 750 Whisper humming away.

Ed points to it. That it?

That's it, Ed, the Mayor says, reaching behind him, patting the console of the server.

He'd be smiling a big, proud smile. Nothing to hide here, Bradley, you self-satisfied jerk.

So basically, Ed says, you've taken your local tax dollars and invested them in porn.

That's right, Ed, the Mayor says.

Government subsidized smut, Ed says, arriving at the title of his segment. You can see it in the glint of his eye, in the way he touches his earring.

If that's what you want to call it, our Mayor says.

Ed says: Do the people you represent *know* what's going on here, that their local government is subsidizing smut?

Yep, the Mayor says, and they benefit from it even as we speak.

Help me to understand this, Ed says. It's the Ed Bradley moment. He drops his head, rests his chin in his hand, looks at our Mayor over his bifocals. He thinks he's got the Mayor in his sites.

Our Mayor reaches across the desk at an innocuous looking pile of papers stacked there. He slides the stack of papers toward Ed.

What's this? Ed says.

What that is, Ed, what you got there is the appropriations recommendation from the federal government, what they say we need for disaster mitigation in the event of another terrorist attack, which the federal government says, Ed, is imminent.

Ed picks up the stack, licks his long index finger, starts paging through it.

How much money do you got in your pocket, Ed? the Mayor says.

Ed hesitates. Excuse me?

Because we need a pediatric defibrillator. You can't use an adult defibrillator on a child, Ed, it'll kill the kid. Most of the classified neurotoxins are designed to do just that, inhibit respiration, so if you're a kid, and you've been exposed to a neurotoxin, you're going to need a pediatric defibrillator, Ed. So how much money you got in your pocket? The kid's poor ma is waiting.

Okay, Ed say, but *porn*?

We're talking an average 377% return on investment, Ed. You show me another investment vehicle with a 377% return on investment, because whatever that is, we're in. We need a pediatric defibrillator, Ed. And they aren't cheap. This isn't a wish list. We need all those things in the recommendations you're holding there. We're talking life and death, Mr. Bradley, not somebody's jerk-off fantasy in Passaic.

But doesn't your constituency have a moral problem with what you're doing? Ed says.

Our constituency has a moral problem with not having a pediatric defibrillator, Ed, and the thousands of other things on that list that we might need in a minute from now.

This equipment, Ed says, nodding in the direction of the Whisper, is funded in part by the state. Do they know what you're doing?

Slick bastard.

Listen, Ed, our Mayor says, right or wrong, the government got us into this thing. They tell us what we need, re: preparedness. It's a governmental mandate, and this is governmental equipment, so we're using governmental equipment to find a solution, re: financing the mandate. You got a problem with that? You got a pediatric defibrillator you can loan me, an atmospheric synthesis unit that's portable?

I do have a problem, Ed says, I really do, Mayor. It's *porn*.

Adult entertainment is not illegal, Ed, not last we looked.

Idea for a public relations campaign: T and A equals Terrorism & Assistance, or something like that. Also, in the event that *60 Minutes* does come calling, alert the local media.

✈ WE PLANTED A MOLE ✈

We planted a mole at this point, so to speak, by having one of us express a keen interest in actually taking one of these yoga classes. We wanted to see just what the hell was going on down there. He arrived late (something about a closing that dragged on and on) and left early; still, we figured we got enough information to get a sense of the thing.

Here's what we found out. The teacher was a foreigner, possibly Indian or a Pakistan, a male of indeterminate age wearing something that looked like a diaper. The soles of his feet looked chapped, if that's possible. He said: Mountain pose, people.

Our man watched the women carefully. When they stood up, he stood up. He did what they did. The air reportedly had a nice perfumed quality to it.

The teacher said: You people in your foolishness want to go to the mountain tops. Okay, he said, so *show* me these mountains. And then he began barking instructions to our man and the women we'd planted him among: Stand with your feet together, your hands at your sides. Your eyes should be looking forward, like the hermit you so wrongly idolize on the mountaintop, looking at the horizon.

You are not the learned people you so desire to be, he said, no, you are not, you are the mountain itself! Spread your toes, open them, then place them back down, one by one as your mountain base.

Raise your chest, he said, raise your head. *Lengthen* your mountain heads.

Elongate your middle fingers, stretch them earthward, and follow with the rest of your fingers into the ground. Breathe, people, breathe your mountain breath. You are the mountaintop, he said, up there alone, your head in the clouds. It's very funny to consider this. You spend your days screaming at each other over what you see as vast distances, from mountain peak to mountain peak. But the further we go down the mountain, the closer the mountains get, do they not? On the valley floor the mountains are connected, are they not? Your mountain base is shared by *all* mountain bases; is this not so? The pressure behind each word that you are screaming, the pressure behind each act that you are acting as a mountain is geologic in its proportion, so vast that you can not see it, but you must acknowledge that it is there, people, you must *acknowledge* it, even though from where you are looking, you cannot see it. You must change this now.

It is funny to think that you think you are alone, he repeated. You must change this.

This is what causes violence, he said. You must change this now for your children, or you will most certainly raise a generation of serial killers.

This was the description of the first pose, the first so-called write-up from the trenches.

Next came something called the Downward Facing Hero, the benefits of which, the teacher said, were relief from fatigue and headache, the reduction of acidity and digestive gasses, the alleviation of menstrual pain and the depression associated with menstruation.

Apparently what you do is drop to your knees, spread them, the knees, and bend forward with your arms outstretched, the palms of your hands and forehead pressing into the floor. The true hero, the teacher said, does nothing. The true hero has disassociated himself from his pain and finds liberation in his silence. Breathe into it.

Press your hands and head deeper into the floor, he said, bow down, give worship to the letting go. You are no longer watching the watch, people — now the watch is watching *you*. Bend lower, press *harder*. Now get up.

Everyone got up.

Corpse pose, the teacher said, walking around the room, handing out long gauze bandages. The stillness is not meditation, people, he said, but a means toward mastery of the inner self, a surrender to that which does not die.

The women sat down on their mats and began wrapping their heads in the bandages, covering their eyes. One by one they lay down. They stretched out their legs and arms. This is when our man had had enough and hightailed it out of there, over to here.

✈ THE SITUATION, IN DETAIL ✈

The situation, in detail, went the general advice, put it out there, right now, just between us — go on now, *shoot*.

Often the women can be bitches, we agreed. We knew by this time that you don't claim something like this unless you're ready to take full responsibility for the sentiment.

You got to *own* the ugly thrust of it, the ugly *bitch* of it, in particular.

It (bitch) bristling like a cornered porcupine, all its quill-like consonants cocked up in provocation.

What was this but goading it on.

What was this but baiting it, drawing the bitch forward, bringing it out into the morning light, an enraged, red-eyed rodent of the genus slut and cunt, such that the words *asshole* and *douchebag*, with their more softening vowels and mounting syllables, sounded so much less abrupt and confrontational, although this isn't being sensitive to other points of view.

This isn't being sensitive to other points of view at all.

Herein lies the problem. You try to see things from a different perspective, the promise being that you'll see your own situation just a little better, and guess what? All your work amounts to a dry pile of nothing much, some stupid, under-stuffed pelt of so-called porcupine, to take the example at hand.

Or worse.

Except now you're just a little angrier and more worn out for the effort. This is basically the fall of mankind, we thought.

How was that for a conclusion to the so-called situation?

A lot of us said we needed time to think about it. There were *a lot* of questions in the air, both big and small, most of them going unanswered.

Question: Are the white cubes in the deli-bought pasta salad cheese (meaning Swiss) or meat (meaning chicken)? Our point was that it's the simple questions that for the moment also got no reply. Why, we wanted to know, should we have to do all the work?

We're experiencing some pretty brutally silent meals, except that the TV's been placed on the dining room table, droning without commercial interruption.

As darkness falls, you could imagine the server down at the DNR uncrated, growing hot, hot, hot with the buzz of commerce. Someone could be down there installing little cooling fans, if the server was ever uncrated.

But there in the dining room, an increasingly silent and suddenly sexless so-called marriage: What was the point? we're wondering.

We were advised that the point was ponderable only when the body is at rest, redirecting airflow.

So put down the shovel, sit down in your seat, the point is love, love, love! We're laughing here.

Those of us working the yoga problem — that growing distraction, by now an all-out imposition, frankly — chimed at this point, saying, Counterpoint: what if love *is* the whole problem?

There's silence all around.

The workgroup continued: The Sutras tell us that when we are established in continence, vigor is regained. Here they held up their highlighted papers as some sort of proof. Says here that celibacy saves energy, they said. In the name of loving and giving, we lose this energy and become mentally and physically depleted. If we are not strong mentally and physically, we cannot regain health.

Someone called for results.

The bad news is we become sick, they said. We might say: When you love somebody, how can we stop giving?

Says here that out of love, we do not know what to give. In fact our love blinds us — it makes us greedy for more attachment. The best we can determine, fellas, is that it's all based on causal logic. Attachment causes us pain and makes us suffer. Our love is just such a so-called curse. Sometimes we even give venereal diseases, thereby spoiling the health of the one we love. What kind of so-called gift is this?

Well, okay then. It was difficult to refute. Giving someone the clap isn't giving someone a dozen roses.

Sexual fluid gives strength and stamina to the brain and nerves, the workgroup continued reporting. Once abstinent, our mind is able to focus without the distraction of our animal instincts to attract a mate, to subdue a mate, to enter into sexual congress with a mate, to procreate, however domestic and normal these activities might seem to be. But it is because these activities are domestic and commonplace that they are so dangerous. If we are celibate for one month, says here, we'll perhaps understand how much of our physical and mental energies are expended in the execution of our animal instincts. It's worth a try, isn't it? Don't bother answering. It's a trick question. Sexual energy is our life. Says here it's where we come from, regardless if the sex act is consensual or not, and where we end, regardless if it's in a bang, blast or whimper. If stored properly, we can distribute the energy and focus it elsewhere.

Oh, brother, were they making this shit up?

No, they said. Says here that by observing celibacy, we preserve not just physical energy alone but mental, moral, intellectual and, ultimately, spiritual energy, as well. Sexual energy that is preserved gets transformed into a subtle energy called *ojas*. There's a word similar to *ojas* in English — ozone. In the early morning, before sunrise, we can apparently go out and breathe the ozonic wind which, it says here, has a special vibration and energy to it. But once the sun's rays fall, this effect is lost. That's why the period between four and six in the morning is called the *divine period*, when the stored *ojas* will make us glow and transmit positive energy. Preserved honey becomes crystallized, just as our sexual fluids gets transformed and diffused.

Somebody said that sure sounds sweet, meaning that doesn't sound sweet at all. That just sounded stupid.

✈ STUDYING THE DOLPHINS ⊁

Studying the dolphins — began a common complaint — every teenage girl's desire, sure, but put the schoolgirl aspect aside for a minute, and throw in the fact that some of us are pretty good with the basic sciences, which includes marine biology, plus add in some more than decent grades in high school science in general, and what you're left with is the fact that there are probably twenty people on the whole planet who actually study dolphins.

Alternatively, there are internships available at the Department of Inland Fisheries.

We're pretty pragmatic by-in-large when there's a living to be made.

There's a little room cut below the embankment of the DuPage River, with a glass window. It's cool and dark inside there. The water is lit. The only equipment needed is a handheld counter. Every time a fish swims by, it needs to be counted.

From here it's easy to daydream about life back on the Earth's surface as a game warden among the trees. What you miss most is sound. Then the DNR slashes the budget for game wardens. Turns out there are maybe twenty game wardens in the entire state.

Then the DNR, like most governmental agencies, is mandated to go paperless. They need a web presence. Office hours, instructions, driving directions. Basic stuff. Local stuff. Can we do it? Sure we can!

Ignorance is bliss. What you don't know about computers and programming won't kill you. That's how every progress is made. There's a moment you pretend to know what you're doing before you know what you're doing. That's how we put a man in space, after all.

Plus, they're paying for the retraining.

You just have to wing it for awhile, whatever, you learn.

After all, the name of the game in biology — molecular, marine, mammal, what have you — is pattern and distribution.

Someone trained to study dolphins or work as a game warden has to have a pretty good eye for the larger forces at work in the ecosystem. It's the same thing for web design — distribution and patterns that give a sense of the larger informational order.

What you do is index and cross-index and alphabetize: *adorable, amateur, Asian, ass.* Bob Lerner, to give another, more specific example, needs to distribute seven hundred fifty units of *Bob Lerner's Guide to Animal Tracking in the American Midwest* in the first two quarters to begin to cover the cost of the dispersal of his information. The unit is discrete. The unit transacted into the broader marketplace takes in the larger system of commerce. It's at this level that we need you to want it, the *Guide*.

Informal surveys indicate that our challenge in creating a marketing push for the *Guide* is that it bores its reader shitless. It's a challenge, seeing the subject is of so little to no interest to most of us.

Of course the subject is of great interest to Bob Lerner, and also the DNR, who was willing to throw an unexpectedly large amount of cash behind it in hopes that it would both become a revenue source and stir up historically low interest in our natural resources and subsequent offices thereof.

All's hunky-dory, except that in a meeting Bob Lerner himself floats animal tracks on Yahoo's main page. Animal tracks, follow them, to *Bob Lerner's Guide to Animal Tracking in the American Midwest.* Sounds good, except for this: Does Bob Lerner have any idea what an invoice for a thousand hits on Yahoo looks like? No.

Bob Lerner tracks his fish right out of the water because Bob Lerner doesn't know caribou crap from content.

Bob Lerner would undoubtedly have an opinion altogether different than the one expressed here, okay, but the fact of the matter is old Bob Lerner doesn't know bear shit from content.

It's *Bob Lerner's Field Guide to Animal Tracking in The American Midwest,* by Bob Lerner, though.

Maybe Bob Lerner knows something about animal tracking, but he doesn't know bobcat cakes about content.

And yet it's conceivable that Bob Lerner might have something to say on the subject, considering he wrote it.

Well, Bob Lerner might know that the ropey-dopey ends of a turd indicates a carnivore — there's a little factoid straight from the *Guide* — but he doesn't know shit, plain and simple, about bringing in traffic.

Bob Lerner's the kind of guy who pays fifty bucks for a haircut, and then tells the barber exactly what he wants. If that's what Bob Lerner wants, why doesn't he shell out seven bucks at EconoCuts, or, better yet, just cut his own damned hair himself?

Who has time for this kind of crap?

Work is busy, busy, busy.

It just doesn't stop.

The stress of such considerations generally makes us long for simpler times.

Historically, we've got your Clothes Folder at an all-night Laundromat, and Fish Tabulator below the banks of the DuPage river. Everyone needs their clothes folded. Everyone needs their fish counted.

The romantic allure of potato farming includes the planting of the potatoes, watering and weeding them, helping them grow until harvest, when the potato farmer gathers them up and makes potato pie, boiled potatoes, potato bread, mashed potatoes and French fried potatoes, just to name a few of the delicious side dishes available to the potato farmer's family assembled to eat at the great table set beneath the yawning shade of some big old trees.

✈ *BURQA BITCHES*, A MEMORANDUM ✦

Burqa Bitches, a memorandum, was circulated by those more involved in R & D around this time. It contained an argument for the development of an adult website based on the following premises: 1) some of us sensing a future where we would need to diversify beyond web hosting alone, and 2) our inkling that a Mideast category might yield impressive numbers, re: traffic.

The idea was simple, the memo went on to explain, and followed the model of *school girls, teachers, secretary, nuns.* We were talking basic fantasy role play, mildly fetishistic, costumes.

The costume itself, with its full closure, made production bone-headedly easy.

A director could put anyone in it.

The so-called model didn't need to be anything to look at, and you could shoot the whole thing in a basement in burbs, or wherever, as long as you had a burqa.

The basic premise was something along these lines: It's shot off the shoulder of the actor. He's a missionary, or tourist, or a soldier, and he walks into the model's hovel.

We're talking a pretty trimmed down set. A table with a loaf of Wonder Bread on it. Maybe you put a hookah in there.

The simpler the more realistic is the beauty of it. We're talking cinder block walls.

Whatever.

Easy-peasy.

A couch.

The actor walks in, the model does that high-pitched tongue thing that you see on the TV news, and then we're down to business.

The guy grabs her, bends her over the couch, lifts her burqa up from behind, and goes to town, either vaginally or anally or both.

At first, she's resisting. But then she starts to like it. You can tell this because the screaming has turned into pleasurable moaning. The money shot takes place on the veiled face.

That was the whole of it.

Reluctant as most of us are to make the transition from web hosting to actual production, it remains at present an opportunity to be revisited in the future.

✈ LET'S DO AN ASSIGNMENT ✈

Let's do an assignment, one of us read aloud from the instructions at this time; let's draw a picture of our significant other. So we drew our pictures of the women, and when we were through, we read the instructions on how to analyze them.

For example, one of us pointed out, what's with this triangle?

We're not what you'd call terrific artists.

One's artistic ability isn't the point here, the instructions said.

It's a picture, we said, albeit a picture that requires an uncommon amount of interpretation. In short, the picture was of one of the wives — in a dress — the triangle was supposed to be a dress, the circle, a head.

Although primitive, now at least it seemed apparent. Someone called it *The Wife: number two pencil on lined paper.*

There's a bug perched on her shoulder, the analysis continued.

Look closely and you'll see that the bug is an octopus, actually.

Certain questions remained. For example, what was she doing in the mountains carrying an octopus and wearing a dress?

When we looked closer, we discovered that it's a seafloor, actually, a rift valley inside an unnamed mid-ocean mountain range, where she was giving herself freely to the octopus.

It's very quiet here, one of us observed, except for the mechanical suck and intermittent burping of a scuba regulator.

We agreed that it was very conceptual, and we put some thought into opportunities to further develop the project — should we, for example, be added into the picture?

Someone who apparently had some expertise in taking pictures suggested that the wife is the only subject in the picture, because, as a rule, he who takes the picture is never in the picture.

It is, however, a drawing, it was remarked.

As a rule, came the reply, he who makes the picture is never in the picture. Plus there is the suggestion of the picture-maker, hence the suck and burping of the regulator.

Then someone pointed out that she's not wearing one, the wife, a regulator, doesn't have to, can't be bothered with such so-called mortal coils that the rest of us must endure: health insurance payments, or regular, preferably monthly deposits into a 401K account to help feed her when she's too geriatric to fend entirely for herself.

The fact that she's underwater explains the squiggly lines, we concurred.

The wife embraces the octopus, and the octopus embraces her.

Question: Why is she underwater?

Because the ocean itself represents her subconscious, someone said, an unnamable ocean because it remains a previously undiscovered topographical feature of her own precious self.

This explains the squiggly lines, we admitted, but not the octopus that she encounters and so quickly offers herself to at the bottom of her ocean.

Its eight arms symbolized to us the eight limbs of yoga, which is most often depicted as a tree, in case you didn't know.

It was, however, an octopus.

Two of the octopus's arms were looped around her shoulder, we noticed, two looped around her thighs, while one followed the crease of her buttocks — you couldn't see this from the angle she's represented — but it hooked around her perineum, flicking at her navel, and the last one, the eighth limb, ran up the back of her neck, draped over the crown of her head, dangled there between her eyes.

Artistic ability aside, the image suggested to us how completely yoga had taken hold of the women. From our vantage point, we felt suspended there, left to look on helplessly while our air tanks went empty.

It was very deep.

It was the ocean floor.

As any old seamen will tell you, someone said here, at seven atmospheres, it's the bends that'll kill you.

✈ THE ANXIETY ✦

The anxiety had been pretty well identified by this time.

First, there's the more so-called holistic fear of the uncertain future our children would be born into. Basically the world is a toilet. What could we say?

The women were telling us to be careful, or the kids will all grow up to be serial killers. We felt bad about that.

We felt pretty guilty about that.

Then there were the more localized fears of drive-by shooters cruising our front porches, pedophiles stalking our sidewalks, Radon gasses pooling in the basement, drunk drivers on the street, arsenic in our tap water, lead in the paint.

Low flying aircraft made everyone nervous.

They'd rotated the flight patterns at the municipal airport again. It was our turn to catch the brunt of descending traffic. What's worse was the low ceiling we'd been having for what seemed like months now, a thick smear of grey that seemed to reflect rather than absorb the lights from the city.

The airplanes seemed to pop out of it, the weather, all at once, and after they appeared, they flew just below it, the sound of their engines echoing off of it as they flew low and slow toward the airport. At night we had to close the blinds and draw the curtains in order block out the chromium leer of the landing lights.

It's getting really hard to sleep.

Meantime, there was a lot of talk about the various injuries and potentially life-ending accidents that our children have lived through. Admittedly, this is the kind of general conversation we can only have from the vantage point of brute strength, of having fulfilled our obligations successfully thus far, full in our dominion over the dangers hunting our children down. One young father recounted how, for instance, baby in one arm and a two-liter bottle of Diet Coke in the other, he had slipped while mounting the stairs of his stoop.

This all happened in a split second of a split second. He dropped the soda bottle and caught his baby by the leg just before its head would hit the concrete step, midair.

We worried about dropping the babies, particularly those of us who were not young fathers. Would our reactions be so quick, our instincts be so keen as to catch our babies, hold on to them and not let go?

So many women in fact were having babies that we decided to buy their gifts in bulk in order to benefit from the bulk discount. We struck up an informal agreement with our Border's franchise owner and secured a gross of *Pat the Bunny* books. When they arrived, those of us who were actually expecting the babies went to pick them up, naturally.

We took them, the books, far away from the clatter of the so-called baristas and the infernal hissing of those espresso machines to the quiet chairs over there near the greeting cards.

It's pretty sweet, truth be told. What other word is there for it? You could imagine that they, the expectant fathers, were imagining that they were carrying their new-born babies in their arms to read to them in that isolated corner of the store. You could hear them getting a little practice in, reading the book through softly but out loud, to see how it would actually sound. When they were done reading, they claimed to feel calmer and not so nearly left alone, as is often the feeling of a soon-to-be father, despite best efforts to the contrary.

It's a terrific little book, that *Pat the Bunny*, sure to evoke a lot of memories, so we were very pleased with our purchase.

In this beloved classic, Paul and Judy play peekaboo, smell flowers, look in the mirror, feel Daddy's scratchy face, and, of course, pat the bunny! All eight activities in this timeless favorite will fascinate your little ones, as it has for over sixty years. Dorothy Kunhardt's *Pat the Bunny* has sold over six million copies and is one of the bestselling children's books of all time, all and all an absolutely fair and square deal, meaning she's *earned* it, as evidenced by the fact that we have a hard time putting the book down, such is its ability to recall that ephemeral state of innocence.

✈ SOMEONE STEPPED OFF THE ✦ RESERVATION

Someone stepped off the reservation at this point, so to speak, announcing the fact over email. The sender's address was unknown to us. We asked around for who wrote it. No one stepped forward. It read:

Been watching the women talking in low whispers at the park. They giggle and sigh. Are they pleasuring themselves in front of me? Their words are like little buzzing rabbit vibrators. Their lips almost touching each other's ears when they whisper! When one speaks, the other looks at her mouth, and then into her eyes, and back to the mouth again.

Their hind-ends hang from the swings, as if they were about to perform the Bengalese Basket Fuck, or they teeter-totter with their legs open wide, their hands stuffed into their open pusses [*sic*]! Up and down they go, up and down, teeter-tottering, teeter-tottering...It's too much!

They hang from the monkey bars as if they were holding onto the heated towel rod in my bathroom, their heads thrown back, stretching, their hair hanging off their heads in big, pullable bunches. They lie in the polymer well of the SuperSlide, starring up into the clear blue sky with their wet mouths open.

You just want to step onto the scene and fuck them all, doggie-style, if only you could remove the children from the set! ☹ *[his so-called punctuation]*

We were alarmed. Someone pointed out the obvious, that there appeared to be a stalker amongst us, that *obviously* someone's off his nut. It was too much for us to handle, so we handed the evidence over to the proper authorities, who conducted their investigation. The language of the messages was closely analyzed. It was determined that the details were too eerily intimate to come from a source outside of us. Interviews were conducted. The field of suspects was narrowed down to those of us with heated towel racks installed in the tub surrounds of our homes, which turns out to be an unusually common feature. There hasn't been a word since, but we remain very, very vigilant.

✈ A DREAM OF OUR MAYOR ✦

A dream of our Mayor around this time involved regional atmospheric scientists interrupting normal weather reporting with brightly lit digital maps that our local forecasters interpreted for him, the Mayor. The local forecasters demanded he prepare for what they called a monumental event.

It's a nightmare scenario, really.

Sometimes nature throws you a knuckle ball, and when nature throws you a knuckle ball, you can't *be* prepared for it. That's why they call it *nature*. Christ almighty, did it ever *snow* in the Mayor's dream.

In the dream, the snow began Wednesday night around eight. The forecasters were saying they were one hundred percent certain that it was going to be very bad, the snow, but there's no way to really prepare for how bad it was going to be. It didn't take long before Mayor knew that it was going to be real trouble. When he looked out the window in his dream, all he saw was white. It was night, and it wasn't dark. It was white outside, such was the volume of the snow that fell in the dream.

So much snow fell in such a short time that the salt trucks couldn't even get out of the garages to get out in front of it. The one or two that did were stranded. The drivers were struck dumb and giddy by the fact. The Mayor could hear it in their voices over the radio (he was manning a radio in the dream): *No go*, he could hear them giggle, we're *stuck*! Never had the Mayor heard such a thing.

When the phone calls came for emergency personnel, there was nothing to be done. Ambulances were stuck in the ambulance bays. The police and firemen were stuck at their stations.

An email from his wife indicated that they, the women, were just now packing their bags and coming home. In the dream they had already left for India, and now he was already dreaming of their return. He told them to hang tight, that we were getting unbelievable amounts of snow. He told them, not now.

We got fifteen feet of snow in less than twelve hours in the dream, averaging thirteen and one-eighth inches of snow per hour, more or less.

So much snow fell that that the weight of it began snapping tree limbs two hours after it started. There would've been a complete communication and power blackout, except our power and telephone lines are bundled with the cable underground, so we still had the power and cable and telephone, thanks to some good, solid municipal planning back when.

The problem was the telephone system was quickly overwhelmed.

EMS was off line. The cops couldn't come. We didn't have any fires in the dream, thankfully, because the fire trucks were useless, even in chains.

Government, what was left of it, operated on snowmobiles commandeered from the John Deere Co-op. It was an emergency. There was no dickering over price. In the dream, we just took them.

The snow was over the eaves of the houses by the time we could get out and assess the situation, which was sometime early the next morning. You'd be driving along on your snowmobile and see what looked like a smoking tree stump in your headlights, but it was a chimney.

It snowed for twelve hours straight, and then it stopped.

By Thursday noon, it looked like most of the whole town was gone, leveled into an almost empty field of white, except for those buildings above two stories, which are not many. In the Mayor's dream, we got into city hall through an unlocked window on the second floor.

Downstairs in the DNR Annex, the snow pressed against the smoked glass windows, which made you feel like you were entering a tomb. It was the quiet, more than anything else. No phones were ringing. That's something you don't see everyday. That's something that just couldn't happen in so-called reality.

Emergency Management set up a situation room upstairs. We had to make a quick accounting of our assets. Phone? no. EMS? like we said, no. Police? no. Snowplows? no. We were in pretty rough shape in the Mayor's dream. Then one of us had an idea.

We assembled in the conference hall where there's a video camera for our live cable feed on the Community Access station. We turned it on and announced the obvious, that we had a situation here with all the snow, but that we were on top it. We acknowledged the fact that the phone system was overwhelmed. It was crucial, we said, that you don't use the phone except to report an emergency. We knew that folks were concerned about other folks — does Grandma have enough medication? are the kids stranded at the sleepover safe? — but we needed to keep those lines clear for true emergencies, life and death, so that if Grandma didn't have her medication, we said, Grandma can get a hold of us and we'll get Grandma's medication to her.

That was the best the Mayor could think to do for the moment, considering the immediate circumstances. Then one of us offered up an idea.

We'd power up the unused server downstairs in the DNR Annex to host a so-called community bulletin board, where neighbors could get in touch with neighbors, where family members could communicate with family members, where we could get a sense of the condition of the community, so to speak.

We had it up and running in a few hours, dream-time, broadcasting that fact on the cable station. Everyone with a computer should post their whereabouts and general condition, the Mayor himself announced. We gave the web address on-air.

It worked. Messages started coming in right off. *Safe and sound. No worse for wear and tear. Buried! but doing alright.* Recipes began to appear, stuff you wouldn't think of, tuna fish pie with Ritz cracker crust, and then there was advice to knock the cabin fever out of the kids.

More importantly, in the dream we could prioritize search-and-rescue to those street addresses we hadn't heard from. We hung the zoning map up and put X's on those plots that were silent.

The upshot is that we were tested. And we made it through okay. In a way it was a blessing, a positive dream. The President himself flew overhead in Air Force One, and designated us a disaster area. And with that, the money started pouring in.

Our budget crisis was finally over, we hoped, so things could finally start getting back to normal.

In the dream, the sun helped. The forecasters were predicting unseasonably warm and sunny skies, which certainly would aid in snow removal, but, considering the amount of snow, would come pretty close to overwhelming our storm sewers. Flooding became a major concern in the dream.

We were definitely watching that water.

What we really needed to do, the Mayor felt, is stop watching the goddamned water and get our hands on some shallow-hulled water craft instead.

We never had temperatures this high at this time of the year when we were kids, someone observed.

What it is is global warming, the Mayor said. It's a damned catastrophe, he said, and then he woke up.

✈ IS THIS A FETISH? ✤

Is this a fetish? one of us wanted to know now. Is there anything more erotic than having someone say you're name while sucking you off?

There was something both abrupt and wistful about the question.

Wistful, yes, we all seemed to agree, a somewhat satisfying sex life, though rather short-lived and infrequent. *Abrupt*, in a word.

The slow and languid mouth is something else entirely.

The true orifice of waste, said Sophocles, or somebody like him.

Still, take your basic soft mouth, the lower lip, wow. The word *lips*.

Yes, wistful, satisfying, good old American middle-aged oral sex.

Camembert softens nicely with age also takes on a nutty, mellow flavor recommended by *Gourmet*.

Question: Why would someone want to hear his name called out during oral sex? In contrast, why not go for some basic low-level dirty talk?

Dirty talk doesn't do much, that's why, inasmuch as it's one-way traffic, so to speak. But hearing your name called out right before you're blown, now that's something else entirely.

Your name comes out from inside her.

Your name comes out of her mouth just as you're sticking your Willy in her mouth.

Your pecker, like a cork, forcing your name back in the bottle, as it were, stopping it from coming out?

Your dick, like a cork, forcing your name back inside the bottle, as it were, and then there's the pleasuring you for the honor of holding your name inside her?

Depending on your point of view, either the clitoris is a very small penis, or the penis is a very large clitoris.

However uncomfortable it was to conclude in this way, we felt that we were, all of us, in this sense, one, inasmuch as having your name called out during oral sex might be of interest to both men and women alike, fetish or not.

One of us posted our conclusion in a so-called chat room on the Internet. It didn't take long for us to get a reply. Imagine marriage as a field of dirt, it went, and you're all standing in the bottom of your individual holes in the field that is your marriage. There you all are, digging. Each of you is standing in the bottom of your individual hole, and your spouses are standing in the bottom of their individual holes; you have a garden spade, she has a garden spade, and here the both of you are, digging like your lives depend upon it. You're throwing spadefuls of dirt, spadeful by spadeful into her hole, but she is trying to dig a hole, too, so first she must shovel out the dirt that you are throwing into her hole, which she does, in an ever-growing pile at the side of her hole.

Question: Are the women not throwing dirt into our holes?

Reply: She is not throwing dirt into your hole. She is trying to dig her own hole, but she is unable to do so, because she is spending all of her energy digging out the dirt that you are throwing in there.

Somebody offered that the ratio seemed skewed.

Okay, so you're in your hole, throwing dirt into her hole, and she's in her hole, throwing dirt into your hole; ergo: neither of you are able to satisfactorily dig your own holes.

We agreed that that sounded pretty right.

Wrong, the flow of information announced: Given the statistical ratio of dirt displacement over time by gender, you're putting more dirt into her hole than she's able to put into your hole. A ratio, furthermore, indicative of your blind selfishness on the matter.

Put that way, the reasoning was hard to dispute. The evidence was ponderable.

✈ WE PROCURED ✈

We procured copies of the *Upanishads* around this time in an effort to understand the proceedings of the women's so-called Book Club, an organization
that we knew to be a covert think tank to further the agenda of the so-called
yoga retreat, the scheduled departure date of which was fast approaching,
and, with it, our apprehension for the standoff that would inevitably, we felt,
accompany it. No matter their argument, we could not let them go.

In short, we needed them to sit still and listen to us for a change, to best
them at their own game.

The Sanskrit word *Upanishad* is composed of the verb *sad*, to sit, with *upa*,
connected with Latin *s-ub*, under, and *ni*, found in English *be-neath* and *ne-ther*.

The whole means to sit beneath something: a person, a tree, a tower, a lamp.

You're supposed to sit in a secret place, in solitude, in harmony with your
soul, master of yourself, free from hope and worldly possessions.

Find a spot that is clean and pure and sit on a seat that is firm, neither
too high nor too low, covered with layers of cloth — preferably deerskin for
some reason, if you can get your hands on some deerskin — amidst some
unspecified sacred grasses.

Are your organs of perception and action finally under your control?
Well, they're supposed to be.

You're supposed to stop looking over your shoulder now. You're supposed
to stop looking into the air.

With your body, neck and head erect, immovable and still, with your
vision indrawn, your sight fixed at the tip of your nose, with your soul at
peace and fearless, you should rest now.

You're allowed to be vigilant, but your controlled mind should be absorbed in the *Me*, meaning yourself, *you*.

Here then your mind is finally under control.

There you have it, the rules of sitting. So if you're determined to sit, sit right. If you want to half-ass it, then you're supposed to sit somewhere else.

Otherwise, absorb your mind in the peace that rests in the *Me*, et cetera.

You don't have to move a muscle.

You don't have to leave this room to find it. It's apparently already here.

Nonetheless, it seemed to be the women's conviction that it would be somewhat easier if you put your self in a different place to find it.

We were advised at this time to take our emotional intelligence back to today's assignment and ask the women important questions to gauge their feelings.

Hey, we asked, why the glowering?

Are you unhappy?

Why the unhappiness?

Does the garbage need to be taken out? The sidewalk need salting?

Is it distance in general and emotional dissatisfaction in particular?

Why the dissatisfaction?

Why hasn't anyone even *tried* to go down on you in over a month?

Is this a fetish?

What does this suggest to you? That someone here is getting some on the side? Do you know that that's not true, that the singular thought is of you before dropping a load down the shower drain, or wherever it is that one holes up to jerk-off?

Don't you get on your knees every morning and thank your lucky stars that we're alive?

Then why the attempt to hide your handwriting here, loosely looped as crochet knots, pinned against the kitchen table with your knitting-needle-thin forearm?

Is it private?

What are you writing?

GO FUCK YOURSELF in big, knotty letters at the end of the paragraph you're laboring over?

✈ PROJECTING OUR FEELINGS ✈ OUTWARD

Projecting our feelings outward, as we were advised to do, meant that the fluffy flakes falling on the green dumpsters outside looked like volcano ash, which suggested to us that our world, this world, is being burned to ashes.

This was the whole significance of the word *ash* here.

The gurgling of the dehumidifiers sounded like the death rattle of someone with emphysema, one of us remarked, the wheezing of the radiators sounded like someone dying of congestive heart failure.

The off-white color of the walls was officially identified as Mushroom on the color palette, for the connotation of burial and dampness. The fabric on all this crappy furniture looked like margarine, suggesting both their shabby greasiness and heart-clogging properties. In this way, our faces equaled fat.

On second thought, the volcano ash falling outside was obviously snow. It covered the earth in bone-white dust.

The Earth's crust is composed of decaying organic matter. A dust storm is, in a very real sense, a shit storm, as opposed to a snow storm, which is obviously just snow. Regardless, we raise our houses on a compost heap.

The heap itself had been described, in a famous poem that someone brought in, as a spent and flaccid scrotum. From the scrotum, in the momentary heat of our virility, we erect our monuments, the poem said. And while some of us began complaining that this was starting to come off as pretty strange, we all conceded that the fastest way to bring your enemy to his knees was to kick him in the crotch. Fighting dirty, yes, but extremely effective nonetheless.

Speaking of which, someone said, let's talk about that aggressive dog at the dog park who, its owner (one of the single women) swears, has been neutered. The dog is massive, an orange mongrel made from Chow and Labrador and who-knows-what. Every time another dog comes through the gate, it displays its dominance by mounting and humping the newcomer. The males, being forced to recognize the strength of this display, reportedly submit and then scurry away whimpering. The female dogs, on the other hand, seem to somehow immediately apprehend the fact of his castration, and no matter how much he growls, or how hard he attempts to mount them, they simply ignore him. In fact, this is how from a distance you can separate the newly arrived female from the male dogs.

There was also a compact terrier brought into discussion that frequents the park, who, you guessed it, has testicles as big as plumbs bulging there beneath his anus. The females surround him, but are careful not to get too near him, in a carefully orchestrated display of deference.

Given all this minutiae, it may seem unbelievable, but no dog has reportedly yet been bitten.

Conclusion: This must be because no one has yet brought a dog with a truly violent temperament to the park. Lucky us. Inevitably, it will happen. How then to formulate a municipal code against it?

✈ AN OPEN COMMUNICATION ✦

An open communication, apparently from the women, was found posted on the bulletin board in the lobby of the Community Center, a highlighted Xerox stating that the principal feature of yoga is the peaceful resolution of the agony of the mind: We are despondent, it said. We're paraphrasing here.

The prospect of divorce creates sorrow. Attachment creates longing.

We remain concerned for your well-being, we thought, no matter the circumstances of your suffering.

In a gesture of defense, they'd probably say that their tears are not shed over our despondency or your suffering, but because some of them have conjunctivitis. If so, the afflicted among them must subscribe to the following prescription if they want relief from their condition.

If flying, first they must recline their seat from the fully upright and locked position and lift their faces to the ceiling of the cabin before applying the medicinal drops.

Once the drops are applied, they will clearly see that coffee and tea service is now being terminated.

Nothing lasts forever!

Metallic trundles like paper-stuffed coffins will eventually be stowed and secured in their proper places.

Everything has its place here.

The *Upanishads* assert that this place where everything exists is the mind.

For example, we are apparently within all, and we are outside all. And their retort: When a sage sees this great Unity and that her Self has become all beings, what delusion and what sorrow can ever be near her? for example.

We'd wait for the women to answer this question and discover after a long and terrible silence that it was a rhetorical question, one that apparently was not supposed to be answered.

Sometime between their asking it and our learning this (hypothetically), we felt that they'd already left us in the lurch.

In the interim, without absolute foreknowledge of their departure, we thought a great deal about the silence. What is the exact quality of the silence? At home, for instance, in the kitchen, this morning.

The refrigerator hums, the heat kicks in after a mechanical preamble, the foundation of the house adjusts to subtle variances in barometric pressure.

This is not silence *per se*.

It's a bleak, unnervingly quiet, kind of the normal everyday stuff of silence.

And yet the stuff of silence is not silence. The stuff of silence is explicitly an un-silence.

There's normal sound: wind chimes, snow blowers, aircraft, something's beeping, the next door neighbor threatening to beat his dog to death.

Silence is generally a loud affair, relatively loud, like the sound of a dripping faucet. It's loud because life is filled with much noise, because it's a very noisy life, listening to the iPod while working, falling asleep with the television on, the maddening tune whistled by the obsessive whistlers among us.

✈ RESTRICTIONS ⤶

Restrictions of the aphoristic form, we soon discovered, made them maddeningly logical.

Still, we were determined to get to the bottom of things once and for all by this point.

Either the idea is the animal, the aphoristic form the mode of tracking (so that if the hunter becomes lost she can retrace her steps backward through the form), or it's (aphorisms) subjecting one's mind to a slow drip of Professional Strength Liquid Plumber. In other words, employed as a caustic agent, aphorisms are apparently designed to burn through the clog of unenlightened consciousness.

Yoga, Pantajali says, is the cessation of movements in the consciousness.

Enlightenment is what is purported to be left there in the scarred, empty casing of the skull.

In order to receive the full benefit of this accumulated acid bath, one cannot skip from aphorism A to aphorism C in the sutra sequence A B C, for instance.

Without the progression through aphorism B, the sutra itself apparently becomes more sewage in the sinkhole of our unenlightened minds.

Hippies once gave the mind mass, calling it heavy.

Aphorisms are designed precisely to flush from its practitioner the despondency of being alive. Consider, for instance, the statement that the prospect of divorce creates sorrow.

Sorrow manifests itself in tears.

An excessive wiping away of tears produces conjunctivitis.

Conjunctivitis is a bacterial infection of the eye.

The bacteria breeding on the organically rich surface of limpid pools creates the following symptoms: combustive burning and itching.

Treatment of conjunctivitis involves two drops of sufacetamide sodium applied directly to the infected eye every six to eight hours.

If the afflicted follows this sutra to the letter, she will be cured of what ails her.

This is the prescriptive, utilitarian power of the sutra.

The problem is stated in the sutra, the problem is resolved, sans baseless whining, without bullshitting around.

Pantanjali asks us to face the facts of our present despondency, but then two-thousand-five-hundred years of recorded despair dumped into the present is not an easily manageable amount of time or despondency.

✈ PHYSICAL THERAPY ✈

Physical Therapy, an idea floated around this time: patients receive home visits for carpal tunnel syndrome.

OSHA calls it an occupational injury, carpal tunnel syndrome, an injury sustained from repetitive tasks, so its treatment is *supposed* to be funded by Workers' Comp. In other words, someone needs to contact Workers' Comp and remind them that they're supposed to be funding it.

No one's married to carpal tunnel syndrome. Take your pick: a herniated disk between L4 and L5 (car accident) or your basic, various replacements — hip (a fall), knee (on the court), elbow (freak shopping cart accident). A case of TMJ, with the man's jaw wired shut (no motive, just a crummy genetic predisposition). There's no talking in this scenario, a least on his end, which makes things pretty interesting!

The physical therapist arrives at the door. She's hot, hot, hot! She's not going to help you into the bathroom to take a leak, no, but she's going to *make you feel better*. She going to give you some *Physical Therapy*.

Maybe she helps you into the bathroom after all. Maybe she helps you into the *shower*, where there's some hot soaping-up action. Meaning, here's your opportunity for some hot foreplay action.

We've got your basic massage that turns into *something more*.

She knows where you hurt. She knows how to make you feel better.

She straddles the bad cases. Hikes up her short skirt. Starts grinding her pelvis into your back.

Ouch!

She's getting pretty worked up. She's got some moaning going on. You can hear it.

Then she turns the patient over. That's when the *real* physical therapy starts.

Where does it hurt?

Lower!

Here?

A little bit lower.

How's this?

Lower!

Oh my.

That's right!

Things get *crazy*. You got the possibility for all kinds of hot physical therapy action, in all kinds of physically therapeutic positions, because, you know, the guy's just *horny*, he's not *really* hurt.

✈ SOME SWAMIS ✈

Some swamis, we learned — this right after learning that the Indian *swami* is the English *person of knowledge*, no more and no less — make it their business to provide the notation of a remainder in a long division problem as r, others provide the largest export crop of Brazil, expressed in kilotons, and still others decree that the most effective rhetoric for baking a bundt cake is process analysis.

Numerous state-supported swamis locate their ashrams at such places as DMVs and DNRs, patiently answering untold questions posed to them from the great faceless petitioner, either withholding or granting license, depending.

I want to burn, it says.

We cannot allow you to burn, we say.

I want water, it says.

You cannot own water, we say.

I want to reserve a campsite at the Happy Glenn Campground.

The Happy Glenn Campground does not exist, we say.

I have memories of the Happy Glenn Campground, it says.

You think.

The happiest of my memories are of the Happy Glenn Campground, so go ahead there, chief, and cut me a pass.

The Happy Glenn Campground exists in your memory, we say, but it no longer exists in this particular, so to speak, state.

Things don't just disappear, it says.

Things are confined to a rusting trash barrel and precisely the land it still sits on, which itself was scheduled for removal ten minutes ago.

You should be ashamed.

Dear sir or madam: your memory is neither recognized as an article of nature nor natural resource, so the Department of Natural Resources is no more responsible for the caretaking of the matériel of your nostalgia than you are for the evisceration of someone else's simple, clean and good desire of making one's life's work the study of muskrat traffic patterns on the frozen marsh — the mapping of their throughways between reedy berms of dry land, the tracing of the borders of their ghettos on the open ice — in order to achieve an understanding of muskrat society far and above your ability to understand your own, however contemptible, however understood in a splendorously snow-white solitude, which inhabits us as we inhabit it, until such time such studies and activities are deemed superfluous, so that one's many talents are instead better put to use in doing your bidding.

I pay your salary, it says.

Gophers and kangaroo rats have underground rooms in their tunnels which serve for latrines, we say. In the drier country of the Southwest, packrat middens may be coated with scat and urine deposits dating back thousands of years.

Our point?

We aren't paid enough to both have the knowledge of that mystery and continue this conversation.

✈ THE SILENT TREATMENT ⤛

The silent treatment sure does put a damper on communication, we said. It goes without saying. Someone accuses you of cheating — at cards, on your taxes, on your spouse — and then takes a vow of silence per earlier discussion, and you've got yourself a problem.

It's impossible to defend yourself against silent judgment, accusations, e.g., question: Prove that your car wasn't parked on 1st and Strawberry way the hell over in Richmond, Virginia, on February 17th. You can say impossible, it wasn't, that you live half a country away, or whatever. Fine. Okay. Now *prove* it.

You got a situation when your Inflatabed is expiring on the living room floor, the floorboards are creaking in the bedroom above, a hot pot of oatmeal is bubbling on the stove, a kettle is about to whistle, an answer to the age-old question demanded: Come on, are you, or are you not, having an affair?

You got a situation where there's an empty pudding cup balancing on the summit of garbage accumulating above the rim of the trashcan in the summer kitchen, an intermittent trail of chocolate pudding that begins there, follows you into the kitchen, ends beneath your left sock, and what you want to know is: Are you fucking someone else? Are you *thinking* about fucking someone else? Otherwise, where's your mind at?

Enough! right?

Isn't it enough that we've a full blown jihad on our hands, that given the chance half the Arab world would cut the head off our President and use it to defile our women and our children? And now this?

We wouldn't move until we got a reply!

We stood there for a long time, torn between the conflicting desire to at once do harm, but also to protect the women. Seconds became minutes, minutes, more minutes. Finally we were forced to concede our position. We left our houses and met at the Lanes. The topic of conversation, of course, remained the women.

Let's discuss their anger issues, one of us said, and how they might be fashioned from incidents in our past, and how the women's sudden devotion to yoga is an attempt to reconcile that past.

Inasmuch as this was sounding like a professional diagnosis, let's be frank here, this diagnosis-making was a source of some uneasiness. So we opted instead to get to particulars, their tendency toward physical abuse, meaning the women's propensity to physically lash out.

Where, exactly? In the bedroom, in the hallway, in the basement once.

On the other hand if what's meant here is not where these incidents occurred, but where on the body the abuse landed, the answer is on the arms, mostly, once on the chest. Does the distinction matter? It does. In American jurisprudence, it is the difference between homicide and manslaughter, which has everything to do with one's intent to do harm.

We are all of us haunted by our pasts, a clique, sure, but the statement doesn't lose its *oomph* by being a clique. Really: What happened to them?

It's commonly known that one-in-four girls is molested before their eighteenth birthday, someone said. The statistics are appalling. Keep that figure in mind next time you're in a room with four or more women, withoor without the wife.

The bar grew quiet.

Then someone asked: Has your wife ever been molested?

You have five women in a room, one has been molested, statistically speaking, is the point.

Has your wife ever been molested? Probably not, but there's something back there — what's the word for it? She retreats into herself, a depression, maybe. A gloomy retreat. Is it depression?

If it's not depression, exactly, then maybe an anxiety?

If it's something much more sedate, something like sulking, but more profound than anxiety, what is it?

Abjection?

A state of utter abjection, yes.

Let's discuss abjection.

This sounded like a diagnosis. Frankly the direction this was going was causing some uneasiness, diagnostically-speaking.

Was it a correct diagnosis?

It was not. Abjection is a descriptor, one of us said, not a clinical category.

✈ WE PUT IN A WORK ORDER ✦

We put in a work order for the CP 750 Whisper to be installed in the mailroom of the DNR Annex. Pretty soon a guy shows up in khaki pants and white shirt. The details of what he's wearing are important because of the way some of us responded to it, what he's wearing, which were your basic, everyday clothes.

We showed the installer to the mailroom, pointed at the server, said there it is.

There's a lot of milling going on in the Annex at this point, a lot of questions, like who's that guy in the mailroom?

He's the server guy, as was already made clear.

A salesman? someone said, obviously not listening.

The *installer*.

He's going to install it? someone said, Dressed like *that*?

That's why what he's wearing becomes important. You've got to point out to the ignorant that the guy's not installing a boiler system. It's a server. The most physical thing he's going to do it take the plug to the outlet and plug it in.

The point's this: Basically it is the first time we're starting to see a little bit of a split amongst us. On the one hand, you got those who've got a handle on the issues. We're looking at upwards to a 377% profit margin if everything goes to plan.

That's what you call a profit center, a pretty damned lucrative business entity, no more and no less, the rewards of which some of the biggest players in corporate America have, as we already mentioned, been reaping for some time now. We just want to take our little stab at our little bit of it.

The grass is browning in the outfield for want of fertilizer, for Christ's sake, to say nothing of everything else.

On the other hand, there were those whose ignorance was bordering on the superstitious, taking and interpreting the Mayor's own dream, for instance, as a sign that maybe we should start backing away from the venture, the online adult entertainment enterprise.

These guys don't know online from a punch line, truth be told, but now they're some real authorities on what they're calling the online porn *biz*.

All of a sudden there's some real tension between us, between, it's safe to call it, the old guard and the new guard.

After the technician left, some of us assembled in the mailroom and had it out, once and for all.

The Whisper was sitting there, black and sleek, its many red lights flickering on and off. It was impressive. For a long time, we just looked at it.

Something like all the technology put into the Mercury capsule that landed on the moon is trumped by the basic calculator sitting on your desk.

Here this thing sat, its intermittent fans whirring on and off, sounding like the thing is breathing, bringing the whole world to us there in that little mailroom.

And in response, we've got nothing. We're drawing an empty blank. There's nothing to see here. Not yet, at least. That's pretty much the agenda of our so-called impromptu meeting here.

There appears the fat folder summarizing our fiscal budget. Emergency Management raises with their report on Terrorism Preparedness that, line by line, tells us what we really need and points to the fact that we don't have it, not any of it.

Plain and simple, someone says, pointing to the obvious, those documents stacked on the server — meaning, the budget and the report — we're not going to get there by investing in T-Bills, gentlemen. We're just not.

Of course we could get there by investing in T-Bills, but not in the way that's going to get us at least some of the basic equipment that we need now.

We're talking portable atmospheric sensors, those hazmat suits, never mind the custom emergency vehicles or bomb detonation devices.

You explain that we simply can't wait for our investments to mature before we test the water where some lunatic has just dumped a ton of arsenic.

The meeting was more drawn out than this. But that's the thrust of it.

It basically ends with somebody saying okay, so what's next.

Everybody's back on board.

Does anyone know how to make a web page?

A few of us do, but this is pretty elaborate stuff. We're going to have to pay for a little offsite consulting, particularly in the writing of code. After that, we can take it from here.

What's next then is that we needed to combine the Emergency Management Budget with the General Budget, render the fat, identify the lean, and job-out the basics of the site.

With that, here we're all back again, on the same page again.

✈ NUMEROUS INCIDENTS ✦

Numerous incidents of excessive cleaning started calling attention to themselves right about now. The dinner table was cleared while the last crumb was falling. There's never a dirty dish that wasn't already done, air drying in the dish rack.

Closets were reorganized, all of them, each and every one.

Stubborn hard-water deposits on the shower disappeared, as had the contents of junk drawers in the kitchen, in the china hutch, below the tool bench, whatever drawer is the junk drawer. The drapes are dustless, the floors shine, the carpet is always damp from a steam cleaning.

For a while it was nice, and we're used to it at certain times of the month, particularly right before the full moon, but this was different. Meaning, it wasn't just limited to those one or two days a month. Exactly put, it was every day.

Then came the reports of some of the women tilting their heads sideways so that they could insert the spout of a miniature teapot into their nostrils. What they did exactly is they poured warm salt water into the upper nostril, blew it out the lower, rinsed and repeated, so to speak.

Packaging found in the garbage suggested the increased use of self-administered enemas. Also there were reports of several of the women caught vomiting in the morning. They, the women, drank several glasses of what's described as saline water on an empty stomach and retched the clear fluid up into the toilet.

Those involved in so-called food-pipe cleansing were seen swallowing what's described as approximately ten-foot strips of cotton cord soaked in milk. This cord was pulled out again, and then a glass of milk was drunk.

Of particular concern, however, were those caught drinking their own urine, which is simply unacceptable.

Never mind the fact that it's pretty goddamned revolting if you really think about it.

All attempts at intervening were met with confrontation. Often objects were thrown: coffee cups, toothbrushes, clothes hampers, the dirty clothes exploding on the bathroom floor. The women rooted through the clothes, calling us dirty animals, saying there isn't enough time or bleach in the world to keep a man's underpants clean.

What they'd do is remove a more worn pair from the heap and wave it in our faces like a flag to our own embarrassment. It's *embarrassing*.

To be fair, the underwear under consideration was never the newest nor cleanest example in our so-called repertoire.

That's probably what you'd call an understatement.

They'd drop it and begin snatching up dirty T-shirts with the yellow perspiration quarter-moons sagging around the armpits, and they began throwing them at us, too. When they finally gain control of their senses, they'd tell us to buy black underwear from now on, or dark blue ones, or any color other than the filthy white ones.

We conceded the point, just another in a long, long, long list of concessions that we felt that we are making and keeping pretty close tack of. We made lists of what's the matter, including: 1) the attack on our homeland, 2) the fact that we won't allow them to go to India, 3) the adult entertainment site under consideration, and 4) that we'd not seen revenue from the adult entertainment site, which goes without saying, considering number three above. With this list in mind, we decided to form focus groups, splitting ourselves into four teams in order to work the four problems.

If a possible solution was found, we reasoned, we'd reconvene to test the proof.

One-fourth of us brought a check home for $50 as evidence that our business was already turning a profit on speculation alone. One-fourth of us offered $100 cash, indicating that it should be put away for the India trip, thereby allowing for the possibility that the trip might take place in the future. A fourth of us simply went home and said that's the last of it, that they we're pulling out of the Internet venture. Finally, there were those of us who brought some cash home and announced that it's going straight to the war effort, or the victim's memorial fund, anything connected to the heinous attack on the United States of America.

Bottom line, the first group, the ones pocketing the $50 so-called profit, tested off the charts.

The findings were reconfirmed by mass-testing, by all of us precisely duplicating the procedure, and things got a bit better for a little while after that.

✈ YOGA ✦

Yoga class, a room full of athletic babes in tights: guy walks in, unrolls his sticky mat in the center of them. Teacher is hot, hot, hot. She calls everyone's attention to the middle of the room, where she's going to demonstrate a new position. Hot yoga action ensues.

How about this: It's all shot through a spy camera placed in the man's eyeglasses. We see the teacher walking towards him, meaning us, the viewer. Tells the guy to stand up. We stand up.

Teacher announces *Triangle pose.*

There's a nice allusion here to threesomes.

Teacher grabs the guy by the ass and elbow, bends him over. Teacher blathers some technical detail, then has the guy stand up. But guess what? Guy has a boner!

We look down, and we see this massive bulge in our shorts. We see our hands flitting around, trying to hide it. We pan around the group of women surrounding us, apparently trying to detect if they have also noticed our huge hard on.

Oh, they notice all right! We got shots of their pretty faces. They're all staring at the package, smiling dirtily, licking their wet lips.

Teacher says: *Oh, my.*

She pulls down our shorts. Women close in like a pack of sex-starved animals.

Question: Why do we have the spy cam mounted in the glasses?

We're going with the trend, following the money.

The question can be fairly asked nonetheless: If we didn't know we were going to pop a rod and be embroiled in a hot yoga sex free-for-all, why are we walking around with a hidden camera on our head?

The camera is hidden *in* our glasses. We're just a guy who walks around with a hidden camera in their glasses, just in case. That's all.

What does this mean, *just in case?*

Just in case there's a hot yoga sex free-for-all, for example. Imagine if we didn't walk around with a hidden camera in our glasses. Imagine what we'd miss!

✈ WE CONFESSED ✈

We confessed a certain deficiency in the skills required to sitting down and talking. We recognize this deficiency, that this restlessness in the face of gravity is a part of who we generally are. We have been amply and often criticized for it, and so we took a page out of the women's playbook and announced that the women themselves could not often sit still for long times, either, despite their insistence on the contrary.

Stillness takes for them a great deal of mental effort, we said. One cannot sit still if one is perturbed.

They were furious.

We said: Perturbation is anathema to sitting still and talking.

In the darkness of our living rooms at three o'clock in the morning on the night they announced their intention to travel, the women shimmied forward on the couches so that their knees could hinge themselves completely over the edge of the cumbersomely deep-seated cushions. We could not see this in the dark but were attentive to this familiar pattern of their movements. Meaning, only in this way were they able to put both bare feet firmly on the floor. The posture implied great seriousness.

The women variously loomed in the darkness next to us, a dark presence, asking for favors. They turned to us, reached through the darkness and cupped their hand on our shoulders.

They put their faces directly into our faces. We're going, they said, but it was more like they breathed it. We'll be back in five weeks. You'll be fine.

We told them to go to hell.

That was real mature.

That's pretty much a summary of how things went. The night the women told us they were going to India there was a lot of so-called sitting and talking in the darkness of our living rooms; for the hearts of lovers facing a five-week separation, someone pointed out, it always feels like four o'clock in the morning. Not to get too sentimental about it.

Most of this in fact occurred at precisely four o'clock in the morning. Thus, it was pointed out, there seemed to be no difference between the inside and outside worlds.

Someone pointed out later that if the yogi, as Patanjali says, realizes that the knower, the instrument of knowing and the known are one, himself, the seer, then all of us sitting there in the dark were already, practically speaking, yogis. A couple of us who had left early to go fishing — they'd blown up the dams on the river, and the salmon had begun spawning again — had arrived at the same conclusion, independently, still on shore, waiting for first light. They, too, seemed to hear the seemingly disembodied voices speaking to us in the lightless space of our living rooms.

We said to the women: Say what it is that you're trying to say. They said that they didn't know if we *felt right*. They regretted nothing of our past, but something didn't feel...*right* about us anymore. Did we know what they meant?

Meaning: Did we have any idea of what they were saying?

We did not.

They said that we seem to have grown apart, moved into separate worlds with separate and unshared interests. The net result is that we had become strangers to each other lately.

Did this have anything to do with our business interests? we asked. Were they secretly angry about it? Given the scope of the project, we had always known that our little capital venture could start to rub them the wrong way, and we had always vowed that if it were to happen, we'd pull a plug on it, so to speak. They said this had nothing to do with that whatsoever.

It was something else.

What? We now told them to go if it meant that much to them. It suddenly became clear how much the trip really meant to them. No one was saying don't go, for Christ's sake, so go!

Here came another bout of the silence.

We said that we thought they weren't the same since terrorists attacked our country. We said don't worry about it, it's all going to be okay, the kid's are going to be fine. They found this latter part offensive.

Talkity, talkity, talk, talk, talk, they said, some silence would be nice for a change.

We were just trying to understand.

At ten past four o'clock in the morning, they announced that they were very near having had enough. Here came the first bout of despondency. Yes, they said, that's it — they said this despondently — they'd good and godamned had it with all of this.

Hey, we reminded them, go ahead and go.

It shouldn't have to *be* this hard, they said.

Question: What did we just say?

We were told that we were free to feel whatever fucked-up feelings we thought we needed to be feeling. They said it was their fault, that they could see this coming all along and failed to do anything about it.

Maybe, they said, they just didn't care enough to.

To what, exactly? we wanted to know.

To do anything about it.

Pantajali says that there are five kinds of mental modifications which are either painful or painless: right knowledge, misconception, verbal delusion, sleep and memory.

They said that, speaking of sitting, they were going to sit on a plane headed for India, just like they'd said they would, just to clear their heads.

One of us said so okay, fuck it. We considered this a painful mental modification. We really were just trying to understand.

They said: And we'll miss them when they were gone.

We thought: This is true.

How, they entreated, did we like *those* bananas?

Not too much.

Patanjali says an image that arises on hearing mere words without any reality as its basis is verbal delusion. An example of this would be the following: His mother was a barren woman, or in the twilight you see a coiled rope and mistake it for a snake, or an emotional depth charge is called a bunch of bananas.

We said can we be, like, *reasonable?*

At least one of the women was in the process of applying for her green card, we reminded them. Immigration would interpret her departure as a violation of the requisite probationary period, we reminded them, so they would have to leave her behind, as well as possibly all the pregnant women, which they acknowledged as a fact — their having to leave them behind — but they, the women who were going, had already received a blessing from them, the women who were staying, for safe travels, and, in return, promises of some good souvenirs.

✈ THE WHISPER ✦

The Whisper CP 750's become an assembly point of sorts around now, a place to congregate informally to talk about our next move.

Often these get-togethers are presided over by our Mayor, if you can say that these meetings are presided over by anyone at all. He has practical concerns. He wants to know when it is that we'll be able to expand storage at the blood bank. He's here to remind us what's at stake. He wants to see some hardcore fisting action on his monitor like immediately, like yesterday, he says, and he says he's only half joking when he says it. He wants to see some serious cash flow last week.

You find yourself lowering your voice around it, the server, almost whispering yourself, although this probably has more to do with the acoustics of the old mailroom than anything else. It's a pretty tight fit — linoleum floors and metal shelving, nothing to absorb sound, so if you use your everyday voice, it takes on volume and sounds a little like yelling.

A good spot, though, all things considered. The server seems to focus our attention on the possibilities before us, on the task at hand, what we come to the mailroom for in the first place.

We don't use it to distribute mail anymore.

Any mail still stacked in the metal shelving is undeliverable for one reason or another. It sits there day after day, molting paper.

That's the problem in a nutshell, the possibilities. There are too many of them. Try to focus on one, to set tack and steer toward something in particular.

Brainstorming, now that's something we've become good at, but then comes the time to tease out the one idea from the rest and follow it through the fabric, so to speak. That's become a bit more of a challenge.

Tracking and trying to steer toward something in particular, these are nautical terms rather than knitting terms.

Meaning, it's pretty soon that the one idea gets bunched up in other ideas, and then it's exactly like you popped your spin casting spool, and all the line gets bunched up together. You spend a lot of time trying to untangle it.

The Mayor wants surplus blood in the blood bank. He wants to see another centrifuge to spin all that surplus blood down. He wants to see a spanking tomorrow a.m., and he wants to be *paid* for it. He's only half-kidding here, he says. Ideas?

We got plenty of ideas. We stand around the server, looking at it, trying to come up with the one thing we can all get our minds around at once and feel good about it so that we can move forward.

For Christ's sake, our Mayor says, let's just slap some tits and ass up and get on with it.

Just slap up some tits and ass. As if. That isn't going to cut it. We want traffic, it has to be something more, something the consumer hasn't seen yet to get us our market share. Otherwise, why bother. The ether is writhing with base fantasies, with blunt nakedness and full exposure made possible by only the most cutting-edge digital technologies.

One of us suggests a specialization in piercing. Clit rings, cockrings, nipple rings, stuff like that.

Anyway.

We're standing around, thinking some more. Then one of us wanders over to the metal shelving, starts absently picking through the mail of some now anonymous recipient, the name now just adhesive backing. He withdraws a manila envelope, frayed at the edges and without a return address. He opens it. Inside is a June 1999 issue of *Barely Legal*. What the hell is it doing here? Who was its intended receiver? Some schlep who didn't want it showing up on the old doorstep, no doubt, who didn't want the missus to accidentally open it before he got home.

Its gaudy cover — a girl with an overbite dressed in a school uniform, her legs spread toward the consumer, just a little peek of her white panties under her kilt — and those slippery pages, already a relic from what seemed to us an unknowable past.

Someone rips out the perforated subscription insert and examines it as if holding a page of a rare, first edition of something or other, a book.

That's what I'm talking about, says the Mayor, grabbing the magazine and holding it up for all of us to see. If these jokers could get their act together back in the so-called dark ages, he says, why the hell can't we?

✈ THEIR OUTBOUND FLIGHT ✦

Their outbound flight to India was a scheduled departure of 4:30 a.m., so by the time *Good Morning America* would be over, the writing would be on the wall, we had to admit it, that the women would by this time have good and truly gone their separate way.

Then there'd come the long and lonely breakfasts for consideration.

There'd be the grinding of the coffee beans to consider, the filling of the Britta pitcher, the watching of it filtering, the buttering both sides of a piece of toast, the throwing of it away, the reconsidering, the taking toast out of the garbage, the opening of the back door, the tossing of the toast onto the snow in the backyard for the squirrels, the watching of the squirrels for several minutes, the watching of the birds, the making of the coffee, the drinking several cups at the kitchen table, the becoming temporarily paralyzed with a fleeting though nearly overpowering desire to hightail it to the Chevron for a pack of cigarettes.

Laudable behavior deserves rewarding.

There would be the resisting of the many maddening moments to rummage through all the stuff left behind.

Resistance, too, gets an exceptional mark for behavior in the exceptional behavior book.

There'd also be the unanswered questions. For example: the word *stuff*.

When we say the word *stuff*, the word *stuff* pretty much equals a cardboard box here, personal effects probably, which would be stuffed deep into the far back of their closets, their name on the label, the word *private* written in black magic marker and underlined.

One box isn't very much.

There'd be the circling of the box for a while after discovering it, the imagining getting caught rummaging through it, the stuff, as if catching one reading through a diary that, who knows if it would be in there, a diary, but if it is, odds are that it'd be in that goddamned box.

Another exceptional mark, behaviorally.

That means something.

How did this feel? A little bewildering, a little numb? A little quiet?

It's already starting to sound a lot like breakfast around here.

What now? Empty bras in the closet, dangling on the rod like filleted pike. All the women's summer clothes would be gone. Numerous remote controls would be reported missing. An empty bookshelf in the bookcases.

There's a difference between the words *departing* and *going*.

Someone suggested the Spanish word *vamos* as a word that graduates the shade of that meaning — between going and departing. But look out that window there, one of us responded, right across the parking lot at that Payless Shoe Source sign, perfectly intelligible despite the snow, because the sign is written in English, planted in good old American soil, and ask yourself here, as you're reading that sign, ask yourself this question: What country *is* this?

✈ SOMEONE SUGGESTED A NAME ✦

Someone suggested a name for our site at this point: *Cum Shot*.

Fine, we said, deferring to the thought put into the matter.

Because the name speaks directly to the center of the business plan, the explanation continued, as if anyone had asked for more explanation: It's like calling a business that sells containers Containers and Things because, along with containers, Containers and Things does, in fact, sell a few things. *That* speaks directly to its target consumer, to the center of its business plan, he said. Who is our consumer?

We arrived at those looking for some porn.

But who is it, exactly?

We didn't know who he was exactly.

Exactly. Let someone else figure out the mean average of female desire. We should know better.

Exactly.

The thinking evolved here toward a boutique of sorts, wherein the cum shot reigned supreme. Meaning, we were going to take the principal strategy of the cum shot and apply it to the spectrum of our consumer's desires. Who gives a crap about context, let's just get in and out, give them the thing in itself, not a single frame more.

Like what, for example?

Demolition footage of stadiums, for starters, high speed water craft at the moment of disintegration, office buildings imploding upon detonation, high speed auto accidents, munitions dumps aflame, bombs destroying their targets, fireworks factories going up in fireworks, flood waters claiming summer homes, avalanches, various sports injuries at the very moment the injury takes place, hurricane force winds ripping off roofs, plane crashes, bomb tests, volcanoes, various folks under fire, monster smoke plumes, various folks on fire, tornadoes tearing into barns, shit in its most abbreviated form, not a second outside the frame of the actual event, not one single frame more, and, of course, various sexual organs caught at the moment of climax.

There was complete silence, so impressed were we with the simplicity of the notion. It was difficult not to let your mind be overcome by the power of the idea, that what we had just possibly heard was the clear plan upon which to build an entertainment empire, a place where all of a man's entertainment needs were available, offered to him in a perfectly tailored, consolidated, almost primitive format that spoke to his most base consumer needs. Even the triple axle toxic spill abatement vehicle in neon lime seemed within reach.

Then someone brought up a trifling little problem called copyright infringement, and that pretty much killed the dream as quickly as it appeared.

✈ THE REAL-TIME TELEMETRY FEED ✦

The real-time telemetry feed on KLM's website was tracking an aircraft in Netherlands airspace, a heading East/South Eastward at 570 miles per hour over Amersfoort.

The general advice indicated that it might be helpful to log off for a moment, as it were, to take a moment to focus emotional intelligence on this issue.

Don't be fooled by those wooden shoes and loamy sunrises, one of us said, the Dutch remain the industry standard in just about every industry conceivable, bub.

Question: Isn't *loamy* supposed to be *gloomy?*

It's loamy here.

Nice content, loamy.

Gloamy is a loamy sunrise in reverse, a peaty sunset.

Look, someone pointed out, it's really snowing.

It was supposed to snow.

It was snowing in Netherlands airspace, although not enough to disrupt air traffic.

As a matter of fact, it's always snowing somewhere in Netherlands airspace.

India on the other hand had become an international warm weather destination, not just a warm weather city, but a warm weather *country.*

KLM advertises four flights to India daily from O'Hare International Airport, and that's just one airport, one airline. Question: How many rupees to the dollar?

It's presently 35 degrees Celsius in Mumbai.

The impulse towards independence is understandable enough, someone said, but it's still difficult not to have romantic notions associated with olden times, however unfounded these may be, so it's hard to feel less than ambivalent over the loss of the city of Bombay, for example.

Being a European-based concern, someone said, you better believe that Celsius is their common unit of measuring heat. Given the ambiguous future of Baghdad, on the other hand, you can have Baghdad.

One of us offered up the city of Madrid spoken by an astronaut in post-launch communications, speaking of romantic — flights to Madrid filled to capacity after the astronaut spoke it. Question: What did the astronaut speak?

Madrid.

Madrid!

✈ THIS COULDN'T BE HAPPENING ✈

This couldn't be happening at a worse time, we agreed. And yet the current literature on the subject suggested that it's never a good time to confront the possibility of abandonment, loneliness and despair.

On the one hand, there was the critical work to be done at work.

Technology was delivering the graphical user interface this very moment.

Speaking about graphical user interfaces, the thing about jargon is that it's exclusionary, which is interesting, actually, when one considers how communist countries rely so much on jargon — Brother Number One, Brother Number Two, and so on.

Some foundational code for our website was complete, as was the invoice for its completion. We were at an important crossroads, materially speaking, meaning, we were closing in on the point of no return, investment-wise.

Question: Was there a Sister Number One in the Khmer Rouge?

Some real bad-asses, those Khmer Rouge.

There's an IBM Selectric somewhere around here, speaking of technology.

The code was complete, the content was expected.

Like, how do you turn this silly thing on, right?

Tech stuff is, like, voodoo.

This probably sounds a lot like taking a Subaru to a loom for tune-ups.

But technology and content, they're two different things.

This probably sounds a lot like having a root canal performed by a hair colorist.

Code is code, content is content, information is inform-ation, or in-forming-ation, minus the —ation part, speaking of information.

Speaking of colorists, what's with that woman suing her hair stylist for twenty-eight million dollars?

Talk about bad hair days.

Content is a whole universe of content in itself.

The thing about content is that as soon as it finds a hole in the dike you're trying to make around yourself, everything pours through it.

Work is something you do — who said this? — not something you are.

It's a full time job, beating content off with a stick. This is the world we live in, like it and lump it. Most of us don't even care about content is the thing, we're just trying to navigate through the space, trying to pass through as fast as we can on our way to something else, dragging our own debris trail of content as we go.

Try to get somebody to slow down and stay for moment — it's a lot easier said than done.

The magic word here is *affordance*, an image of an infant sitting in the center of a rifled-through *Tribune*, the Sunday edition, the image of the infant stunned beyond crying. The word here is *affordance*.

You get these people hanging out, knocking back a couple of dirty martinis, evaluating a graphical user interface.

You get the term *affordance* to refer to the qualities of the physical world that suggest the *possibility* of interaction relative to the ability of an actor — person or animal — to interact. Does the user perceive that clicking on the object is a meaningful, useful action, with a known outcome? asks the deep, dry, dark center of Palo Alto.

The question of whether or not this is a nice place to sit is a classical, deeply complicated affordance question, including all the implications of the environmental, cultural, instinctual issues that shape the mental model of our understanding and expectations when we interact with, in this case, a chair.

We have learned to click on underlined things automatically, which is a big step.

✈ EVIDENTLY, EVERYTHING'S DESIRE ✦

Evidently, everything's desire, we learned now. The Vedic pundits in the *Upanishads* deem this the fundamental problem. Our actions are dictated by the pursuit of our desires.

What pathologically optimistic and bright flight attendants perhaps desire at this moment is to make a fully-orchestrated pass up their assigned isles. This pass is their absolute function, what they have been preparing for since their ascent into the airspace somewhere above the Netherlands.

Citrusy scents must waft from flight attendants' rear-ends as they dole out thin pillows from overhead compartments, drape thin blankets over cold shoulders and exposed, bare thighs while darting fore and aft for last requests.

If you desire water, a flight attendant will eventually appear, carrying a plastic cup of water.

Other passengers would want other things. Thus the cabin of KLM Flight 1181 would be humming with competing desires, all of it expressed in garish ambient lighting.

Unable to function otherwise (if they functioned otherwise, they would be captain, passenger or ground crew), brightly scented flight attendants would be dispensing tomato and orange juices and rich, amber colored cocktails before they themselves would settle into their seats for the long, overnight leg between Amsterdam and Bombay.

The previously unfathomable distance from here to India is some 8,000 nautical miles, more or less.

For the moment, then, we hold onto our memories of the bodies hurtling through space.

Our memories, Patanjali says, all of our memories are the unmodified recollection of words and experiences.

Here's some fragment of a wholly irretrievable memory of late summer, about as vivid as the weather forecast for a uneventful Wednesday late last year (but which smells vaguely of cotton sheets and Vic's mentholated vapors, and sounds, vaguely, like a summer cold).

The images of the fall just lived are likewise an insubstantial montage of moments without any ordering by importance: a shoeless child crying sop-footed in the street, for example.

Here's the empty sneaker stuck in the grate of a sewer drain.

Here are four, cold tater-tots on a white, ketchup-smeared plate, the unmodified recollection of the word *tater-tot*, a figure in cool shadow, standing across the yard in late March twilight, one hand on the backdoor knob, the other hanging earthward at the wrist, unoccupied.

The Austrians have a saying, something about nostalgia being the brain's Chlamydia. We're looking for attribution.

It's probably in a book in that box in the closet.

It's an interesting statement, philosophically, a good one-liner, *gratis*, for a dinner party when you don't want to seem too shallow, when you want to seem like you have at least half a brain.

✈ THE INABILITY OF HISTORIANS ✦

The inability of historians to pin down a more precise date for the origin of *The Yoga Sutras* apparently stems from a controversy involving whether Patanjali was a single person or several persons working under the same title, collaborating on the sutras over space and time.

An uncontestable fact, however, is that the aphorisms and the sutras they comprise are among our earliest formal compositions.

Written language itself originated in Mesopotamia around 3200 B.C.

One of our sources states that the most recent and influential practitioner of aphorisms is the Austrian philosopher Ludwig Wittgenstein, in particular his *Tractatus Logico Philiosohpicus.*

Wittgenstein's use of aphorisms is valued for being completely and utterly revealing.

It's as if each of Wittgenstein's aphorisms is Wittgenstein himself reaching into his rough woolen trousers, slapping his scrotum onto the table for examination so that we may contemplate each vein, each minute wrinkle, hair, the very follicle from which each hair sprouts.

We are, of course, free to reject any one of Wittgenstein's propositions out of hand.

Wittgenstein can assert that each atomic fact contains within it all atomic facts, and we can say: Nice try, Ludwig, but we don't *think* so (and still, it is *unnerving* to find one so open, his overtures so bald, his posture so defenseless, his angular countenance so unclouded, his sullen cheeks a little rouged…).

We find Wittgenstein sitting just so on a threadbare, faded pink Queen

Anne in a windowless room, listening to Mahler's *Das Lied von der Erde* while simultaneously recalling two youths from his boyhood.

Our two youths lead two horses, Wittgenstein says.

The two horses are grazing on the white and purple lilies growing sporadically on the side of the road.

One of the boys leading one of the horses, Wittgenstein confesses, is himself.

The gramophone record of the symphony, Wittgenstein says, the musical thought, the score, the waves of sound, are all inside one simultaneously.

The gramophone record, Wittgenstein says, the musical thought, the score, the waves of sound contain each other's logical structure, just as the two youths, their two horses and their lilies are assembled by identical atomic facts.

Wittgenstein concludes that they were all, in a certain sense, one.

In a certain sense, we are, of course, free to tell Wittgenstein to stop harassing us here, to say unambiguously that we flatly reject his advancements.

No means *no*, Ludwig! And if we do reject any one of his propositions, his whole gesture then groans under the weight of its collapsing structure, leaving poor Wittgenstein with his rough woolen trousers slung around his ankles, his decisiveness shriveled, drained of all that bold blood, inching its way back toward the spine of his treatise, his plaintive, wondering eyes searching behind us for the source of his shame.

✈ JUST AS WE SUSPECTED ✦

Just as we suspected, a pretty exhaustive study conducted at this time by Fulcrum Ltd. and Public Radio indicated that 82.5% of American males aged 18 to 40 accessed Internet pornography at least once a week; 33.6% of American females in the same age group were reported to have accessed Internet pornography at least once a week. What did this mean? It's obvious. More than half of us were accessing Internet pornography, that the accessing of Internet pornography had become a mainstream, so-called *populist* activity.

Statistically speaking, odds are that if you're 18 to 40 years old, you're accessing Internet porn and we're accessing Internet porn — we're all of us, statistically speaking, accessing Internet porn, although given the relatively narrow scope of the study, certain extrapolations needed to be made to account for broader demographics.

Our thinking through our business plan was taking in and adjusting for this information.

The implications of these findings were encouraging, to say the least.

The study went on to confirm what we already knew, that the category receiving the most traffic was indeed the *cum shot*, itself a relatively early subclass in the online sex environment, behind more traditional visual fare, which was simply produced by VHS cassettes transferred to digital format (*Behind the Green Door, Debbie Does Dallas*, etc.) and downloaded.

We were definitely out in front of it in terms of naming our site.

The study also revealed what we already suspected, that oral and missionary sex scenes were now almost entirely edited from their broader context and offered under the categories of *blow job*, for instance, and some form of *fucking*, so that we definitely felt that we were out in front of the form, as well.

The report identified the trend that the sudden, widespread availability of digital cameras allowed a producer to focus on creating a product that appealed to the more narrow and fetishistic tastes of the consumer, tastes which were historically too narrow in their interests for a producer with mass-market ambitions.

This is becoming a little repetitious, but the point needs to be made.

Also, as more and more of us were accessing Internet porn as a primary or secondary source of entertainment, the form of the porn clip, the *teaser*, went from a marketing tool to feature entertainment. Why? Because it's *free*. We saw this coming a mile away. We had already forecast as much back when we were investigating the possibility of setting up our little consultancy business.

So what, right? So we were not going to make money on membership fees. We were going to make our money on the amount of traffic and advertising revenue. Get in and get out.

We've stated all this before.

We got no more time, is the thing. That's the final analysis.

That's the thing, plain and simple. Are you going to deny that? But listen, you got a couple of minutes?

We all got a couple of minutes, maybe not a lot of time, but we got a couple of minutes, and we spend half our damned lives on the computer already anyway, don't we? We sure do.

At least more than half of us. The other half is getting on the computer while the other half's getting off. So you got a couple of minutes — what are you going to do with it? Read a book? Watch TV? You're sitting there in front of the computer all day already, watching TV. What do you want, *more* TV? No, you want some *entertainment*, that's what you want. There's nothing more entertaining than sex. Earth shattering news, this isn't.

That's what it's all about. But what do you have, maybe a couple of minutes, right? You're going to waste your time with all the stuff that leads up to it, or what? No. You want it right now, is the thing. And besides, pornography is pretty much your *Reader's Digest* condensed version anyway. You got your short build up, et cetera, as per earlier examples.

That guy who's thinking about the cum shot is thinking about the cum shot long before he sits down in front of the computer. He's on the bus thinking about that cum shot. He's reading the lists of names of the dearly departed in the newspaper, but he's thinking about that cum shot waiting at home for him. He gets home, kisses the wife and kids, finds himself a little privacy in the basement, he surfs around a minute or two until he finds the thing he's after, and then afterwards he goes upstairs and throws a few lawn darts before dinner. Life goes on.

It's the way things are heading. The problem is trying to keep a market share. Take those couple of Arabs, they sure as hell knew what they're doing. How are you supposed to compete for time and attention against such a spectacle? That's what they call a basic problem of suppressed product identity.

✈ TO BE FAIR ✈

To be fair, if it should happen that the women are found absent, or in anyway unavailable to defend themselves, a defense will be mounted on their behalf. Often they aren't painted so rosily.

One gets the sense that this is not going to be very productive.

On the issue of hygiene, they are admonished for their pores. A joke that'll be said about them in their absence is that their pores are so tight, if a kid licked their forehead on a freezing day, the kid's tongue would get stuck on their forehead (incidentally, if they hate the cold, it would be reasonable to leave the cold — but are they actually thinking of returning as late as spring?). They are scrubbed so clean, it's been said, that they've finally scrubbed their eyebrows off. They operate within a conflicting aroma of astringents and Fitch's Chamomile Soap — who knows who came up with the name of the soap.

This display would probably lower their opinion of us here, not the content of what's being said, but the motives for saying it. This is understood.

In brief, then, here's an example of what happened today, if they were not here to experience it: A pizzeria opened, a dwarf spoke with a falsetto voice, a cosmetics consultant was caught embezzling and investing heavily in Yen. Also, a sheriff out in the countryside found a grandmother in her bathtub. There was a pillow under her head, a collection of fashion magazines piled up on her breast, a half-eaten chicken salad sandwich on the rim of the tub. What she did was disconnect the propane hose from her bathroom heater. For an old lady, you have to admit it, her mechanical aptitude was impressive.

There were a lot of lines everywhere, which was aggravating. We need to keep reminding ourselves of perspective. When detained, as if the long line at the bank or airport security suddenly feels part of some secret CIA detention center, for example, we think about that guy in the *Argentine National Commission Report on the Disappeared* who testified that if we thought for one moment that *sitting hooded, all the time* is just a figure of speech, we should think again. This was not the case. Prisoners were made to sit on the floor with nothing to lean against from the moment they got up at six in the morning until eight in the evening when they went to bed. They spent fourteen hours a day in that position. And when he said *without talking or moving*, he meant exactly that. They couldn't utter a word, or even turn their heads. On one occasion, a companion ceased to be included on the interrogators' list and was forgotten. Six months went by, and they, his captors, only realized what had happened because one of the guards thought it strange that the prisoner was never wanted for anything and was always in the same condition, sitting there, hooded, without speaking or moving, for six months, awaiting death. Now ask yourself: are you in Argentina? No. So we take a breath, put our heads down, and push on.

In closing, last night's dream. Imagine coming home from work and finding a turd in the toilet! We open the toilet lid, and there it is: large, reddish-black, cylindrical and ropey with tapered ends, what's called nipple-dimple ends. The turd is characteristic of a carnivore. You, dear, are a vegetarian, an herbivore. What are we to think? Coprophagy is the process by which mammals re-ingest their own scat for nutritional value, Bob Lerner says. If only. Had you any visitors today? Any at all? No visitors, you say, *why?* What's more disturbing, the thought of someone coming to the house to fuck your spouse, or his taking a dump in your bathroom afterwards?

Post script: We'll be revisiting the painful history of penises this evening, with regard to the comparison of penises to other penises. The subject had evidently not been exhausted before it was dismissed unfairly. It's true, some prefer the word *exhausted*, some the word *dismissed*, but feelings remain hurt, and so the subject has evidently not been exhausted. When penises are compared to other penises, the subject is not so easily exhausted.

There have been apologies, true, but apologies have been a matter of decorum, empty.

To be fair, perhaps this issue is not one penis compared to a past lover's penis, but more generally the inability — or unwillingness — to satisfactorily stave off ejaculation.

This is not the point. One expects to come out on the winning end of these things, always, that's the deal.

Question: Would that have mattered? Does the difference between an insult and compliment matter? It matters. So it's possible that this can be boiled down to something very uncomplicated — something at the animal-level, something very primitive, is all. Better penis, a more avid sexual partner, perhaps rendezvousing in India with a past lover, while those who are left sit at home all alone, in silence, watching the water filter.

✈ FLIGHT 69 ✦

Flight 69. We're sitting on the isle. We glance down. The tray table is down, covering our lap. We're on an airplane, in the cabin of an airplane, Flight 69.

Maybe there's an in-flight movie playing. Maybe that's the part of the flight we're on.

That's fine. We glance up, see a severe looking flight attendant, one of those broads as frigid as winter, all buttoned up with hair pulled back tight. She scowls at us.

Things aren't looking too promising here, what with the severity and the scowling and such.

She's grimacing.

That's not very nice.

Suggestion: The in-flight movie could be a porno.

The intricacies of such a scenario are probably too prohibitive. How did the porno get installed on the in-flight entertainment system in the first place? That's just one for instance.

Sounds like the makings of a comedy here.

We glance to the right, in the direction of the window seat, where sits a truly hot babe, putting dollops of hand cream on her hands, rubbing it in. She's got those glass earrings on that hang really low, which always look so nice. She smiles.

Now we're talking.

We say hi. She says hi. We say where are you going, but we drop the word *are*, so that it comes out *where you going*, almost in a whisper, the effect being some kind of foreign accent. She says on vacation. Ha, ha, we laugh. We meant: where are you going, meaning what's your final destination?

Maybe she just didn't understand, what with the accent and all.

What are we talking, someone along the lines of an Arnold Schwarzenegger?

Arnold Schwarzenegger sounds something like Henry Kissinger.

On vacation, she says again, drawing out the word vacation this time. With that, she snaps the lid of her hand cream shut. Those earrings dangle, glass ones the color of honey, that really sexy pair. What about you? she says. We're staring at her jugs at this point. They're not too big and not too small. Just natural, just *right*. Business, we say.

Yeah, *business*.

Glance down to the tray table, lift it up; we've got our huge cock in our hand! Surprise! And something in the other hand, too. Guess what?

A gun!

Problem: you can't bring a rifle on a plane.

That's why it's a pistol.

Watch out! What pistol?

Hot babe next to us looks into our lap, drops her hand cream, look of horror on her face. Is it the monster cock pointed in her direction that frightens her? the gun? In her face unfolds the instant truth of the matter: This shit's going down, bitch, *and so are you!* We reach out and grab her by the arm, force her to stand up.

Things are getting pretty complicated here, but not necessarily in a bad way, which isn't meant as a criticism, no kidding, but simply as an observation. What's next?

What's next is we kind of drag her to the front of the aircraft where the severe looking broad would've shown us how to adjust our seat belts and, in the unlikely event that the cabin would depressurize, strap on our oxygen masks. The point is that we're taking control of the plane, goddamnit, taking control of Flight 69. We grab the intercabin telecom unit and announce the fact.

Pretty complicated stuff, obviously, not the least of which has to do with basic set design, is all.

We announce that we're taking over the flight, that you American bitches, exporting your lust and various so-called degradations and seductive ways — something along these lines, we'll work on the language — now you will see what it means to get fucked!

Shazam!

With that, we motion to the glowering flight attendant with the barrel of our gun. And you, we say, you come here. She comes. We're nervous. You can tell this by the way we keep glancing at the passengers, the approaching flight attendant, and the hot babe, as seen through the secret camera built into the frames of our glasses. It's difficult to know what to do with the flight attendant now that she's here, but here she is.

Maybe the flight attendant is the only one who speaks our language. Maybe the flight attendant has to translate for us. We say, Tell the hot babe to take off her pants, and the flight attendant says something like: Miss, you must take off your pants, et cetera.

That's pretty hot. Now tell the hot babe to take off her shirt.

Miss, you must take off your shirt.

Now take off that bra. And those panties.

But keep the earrings.

And this to the flight attendant: Take off your flight attendant hat, let that hair down.

Right. She's got that steamy librarian thing going on. She takes down her hair, and guess what? She's super hot, too.

Here's what's next. What's next is that we pick the babe up — the passenger, not the hot, at this point, flight attendant — and we turn her over in mid-air, so that her legs are pointing straight up like fireplace tongs, her earrings dancing in the center of her sexy ears. We spread them, her legs, and lick her pussy! We tell the flight attendant to tell her, the passenger whose pussy we're licking, to reciprocate, which she does, at first hesitantly and in great fear, but she must do it to save the other passengers, and *voilá*! A standing 69 — hence the title.

In the absence of the ability to build the set, does anyone know where we can get our hands on an airplane for a couple of hours?

This isn't the end, not yet it isn't. We're standing, our arms around hot passenger babe's torso, she's sucking our cock, and we have her upside down, standing, her legs straight up, we're sucking her snatch. Thus engaged, we frequently eye the other passengers suspiciously. But they, too, are getting horny. There's a lot of lip licking. We wave the gun. We say get fucking you American sluts! That's all it takes. All at once there's a swarm of groping going on. It's a fuckfest at 30,000 feet! After we cum for the first time, we set hot passenger right side up, grab her earringed ears, give the babe a deep old sloppy frencher that's fully returned, and we're ready for round numero two.

Okay, cut.

Cut?

We've just blown our load in her mouth, and now we're going to kiss it? No way, Jose. That's just nasty.

That's not nasty, someone says after some reflection, that's just *sick*.

✈ PATANJALI SAYS ⤛

Patanjali says that yoga is the cessation of movement in the mind.

Apparently, for a keen student, this one sutra would be enough because the rest of them only explain this one.

If the restraint of the mental modifications is achieved, one has reached the goal of yoga.

Rational people just don't *do* the things we're doing.

We seek out our suffering nonetheless.

We seek out equitable endings to this madness.

We will not let this go unfinished, and wherever you are, you must know this.

We have done so before.

We will do so again.

One learns from one's history.

Patanjali says history is an illusion.

History is the accumulation of unfulfilled desires, he says.

What we want is to stop wanting.

This desire, too, is a want.

Therefore, history repeats itself.

The history of love is in the attempt of lovers to reconcile their wanting something different from their beloved.

This reconciliation is typically a voluminous process, filled with both emotional and physical injury.

Yet in silence, Petanjali says, the self abides in its own nature.

And yet when — the thoughtful man must consider — is the appropriate moment to sit down at the kitchen table and read through the catalogue of one's grievances?

When his marriage is possibly already over?

This question serves no purpose but to inflict more pain.

The reasoning goes that accepting pain is usually misunderstood, because it translates into masochism, when actually it should stand for something else. Accepting pain here means to burn or create heat. Anything burned out will be purified. The more you heat gold, for example, the more pure it becomes. We will actually be happy to receive pain if we keep in mind its purifying effects. Pain here also refers to self-discipline. Although control of the senses and organs often seems to bring pain in the beginning, it eventually ends in happiness. Welcome the pain. Thank the people who cause it, since they are giving us the opportunity to steady our minds and burn out impurities.

As if.

Through cultivation of friendliness, compassion, joy, and indifference to pleasure and pain, virtue and vice respectively, the consciousness becomes favorably disposed, serene and benevolent.

One day winter will be over and dusk will finally come, and the balmy breeze that had been blowing all day will briefly shift from the Southwest to True South, pushing with it the traffic noise from the bypass ringing the city, and then it will die down all together. The early spring night will be uncommonly warm and wet. Windows will be thrown open up and down the block. The force of the transition will seem to demand silent observation, and for several minutes, nothing will stir, the streets remaining motionless and empty, except for the yellow taxis that seem to silently coast down the street and stop in front of various houses, the occupants who have lain down for a nap in the afternoon, will have apparently overslept and are sleeping still before a whirring box fan, until they feel a hand wordlessly touching their heads. They draw up in alarm. In this way they are awakened.

✈ TRAVERSING NEARLY ✦
UNIMAGINABLE DISTANCES

Traversing nearly unimaginable distances will take perseverance and good fortune in equal measure.

If the seat next to one of the women is vacant, for instance, it will be a miracle. If the seat next to one of the women is vacant, it will be littered with fashion magazines, wads of tissue, cellophane bags of stale fruits and nuts purchased at an airport newsstand to keep the blood sugars elevated, a small plastic bottle of sulfacetamide sodium. She'll squeeze out luxurious, light orange ribbons of peach scented hand cream on chapped hands, apply bcc's wax to her dry, full lips.

At thirty thousand feet, at an airspeed of 450 knots (more or less), she'll peer through the inky darkness, down at an earth that faith alone insists is still there, upon which lives are still being lived in ordinary, more earthbound fashion, including our own.

Down there, husbands and wives and children are sleeping well on the ground.

Sleep alludes the despondent in the air.

We are here, sleeping on the ground.

Unencumbered by the presence of our spouse's body, our limbs are allowed to stretch to the four corners of a comfortable mattress.

This good mattress exists in a simple, comfortable bedroom.

This good bedroom exists in a small, comfortably modest house in the north-central region of the United States of America.

This north-central region of the United States of America is the safest geographical landform in the entire world, insulated from earthquake and invasion alike.

We are nonetheless destined to sleep restlessly, skipping like a stone across the surface of erratic dreams in a sleep made shallow from drinking too much cheap Merlot and eating too few canned raviolis.

We lie in bed perplexed and grieving, but tired, too (blame the wine or the grieving or perplexion).

We are here on the ground, reading outdated copies of Fromme's *Visitor Guide to the Mysore Palace* (1963) and cross referencing departure schedules, some of us perhaps preparing ourselves to follow our wives' contrails into the mystery of their silences to India, where we will demand their safe return.

For every action there is reaction.

The enlightened husband might therefore say: Bullshit. If this is an illusion, then we will not lift a finger to do a fucking thing

The women, on the other hand, may well secretly desire action. This accords with the activities of their minds. Their minds are moving very rapidly, though their bodies are still. This, too, is an illusion. The women's bodies are presently being hurled through the sky, back home to us, at nearly the speed of sound.

✈ ABOUT THE AUTHOR ✈

Christopher Grimes is the author of *Public Works: Short Fiction and a No-vella* (FC2, 2005). His stories have appeared in *Western Humanities Review, Beloit Fiction Journal, Reed, Cream City Review, First Intensity, KNOCK,* and elsewhere. He teaches literature and fiction writing at the University of Illinois at Chicago.